A Note from Enid Blyton's Granddaughter

Welcome to the new edition of The Famous Five series by Enid Blyton. There are 21 books in the collection, a whole world of mystery and adventure to explore. My grandmother, Enid Blyton, wrote her first Famous Five Book, 'Five on a Treasure Island' in 1942. That was in the middle of World War Two (1939–1945). In the story, Julian, Dick and Anne meet their cousin Georgina and her dog, Timmy, for the first time. They soon learn *never* to call her Georgina. Together they explore tunnels and caves, discover hidden passageways and solve crimes.

I first met the Famous Five in a recording of 'Five have a Mystery to Solve'. Julian, Dick, George, Anne and Timmy have developed a love of sausages and can't seem to get enough of them. The sausages are put on hold when a lady knocks at the door of Kirrin Cottage. She has come to ask if the Five could keep her young grandson company in a remote cottage while she is away. The adventure begins as soon as they see the mysterious 'Whispering Island' as they cycle to the cottage to meet the grandson, Wilfred.

Timmy has always been my favourite character. He is the best judge of personality and when he is around, everything seems much safer; not that I am scared of adventure! Since watching the Famous Five television series in the 1970s which cast Timmy as a Border-Collie sheep dog, I have always wanted to have a Border-Collie.

Who do you think you'll like best?

Sophie Smallwood, 14 June 2010

Five On A Treasure Island

Enid Blyton

THE FAMOUS FIVE

Five On A Treasure Island

Hodder
Children's
Books

A division of Hachette Children's Books

Contents

1 A great surprise

'Mum, have you decided about our summer holidays yet?' said Julian, at the breakfast-table. 'Can we go to Polseath as usual?'

'I'm afraid not,' said his mother. 'They're full up this year.'

The three children at the breakfast-table looked at one another in great disappointment. They loved the house at Polseath, and the beach was perfect for swimming.

'Cheer up,' said Dad. 'We'll find somewhere else just as good for you. But Mum and I won't be going with you this year. Did Mum tell you?'

'No!' said Anne in surprise. 'But . . . you always come with us on our holidays!'

'Well, this time Dad and I have planned to go to Scotland,' said Mum. 'Just the two of us! You're all old enough to look after yourselves now, and we thought you'd love the chance to have a holiday on your own! But now that you can't go to Polseath, I don't really know where to send you.'

'What about Quentin's?' said Dad suddenly. Quentin was his brother, the children's uncle. They had only seen him once, and had found him a bit scary. He was a very tall, frowning man, a clever scientist who spent all his time studying. He lived by the sea – but that was pretty much all that the children knew about him!

'Quentin?' said Mum. 'What made you think of him? I shouldn't think he'd want the children messing about in his little house.'

'Well,' said Dad, 'I bumped into Quentin's wife in town the other day, and I don't think things are going too well for them. Fanny said that she's thinking of getting a lodger for a while, to bring a bit of money in. Their house is by the sea, you know. It might be just the thing for the children. Fanny's very nice – she'd look after them.'

'Yes – and she has a child of her own, too,' said Mum. 'What's her name – something unusual – yes, Georgina! How old would she be? About eleven, I should think.'

'Same age as me,' said Dick. 'It's strange to think we've got a cousin who we've never met!

She must get lonely all by herself. I've got Julian and Anne to play with – but Georgina is just one on her own. I bet she'd be glad to see us.'

'Well, your Aunt Fanny said that Georgina would love a bit of company,' said Dad. 'You know, I really think that would solve the problem, if we ring Fanny and arrange for the children to go there. It would help Fanny, I'm sure, and Georgina would love to have someone to play with in the holidays. And we'd know that our three were safe.'

The children began to feel excited. It would be fun to go to a place they had never visited before, and stay with an unknown cousin.

'Are there cliffs and rocks and sandy beaches there?' asked Anne. 'Is it a nice place?'

'I don't remember it very well,' said Dad. 'But I'm sure it's an exciting kind of place. Anyway, you'll love it! It's called Kirrin Bay. Your Aunt Fanny has lived there all her life, and wouldn't leave it for anything.'

'Oh Dad, ring Aunt Fanny right now and ask her if we can go there!' cried Dick. 'Please! I just feel as if it's the right place somehow. It sounds sort of adventurous!'

'You always say that, wherever you go!' said Dad, with a laugh. 'All right – I'll ring up now and see if there's any chance.'

They had all finished their breakfast, but they waited while Dad went out into the hall to telephone.

'I hope it's all right!' said Julian. 'I wonder what Georgina's like. Funny name, isn't it? More like a boy's than a girl's. So she's eleven – a year younger than I am – same age as you, Dick – and a year older than you, Anne. She ought to fit in with us all right. We'll have lots of fun!'

Dad came back in about ten minutes' time, and the children knew at once that he had good news. He smiled at them.

'Well, that's settled,' he said. 'Your Aunt Fanny's delighted about it. She says it will be good for Georgina to have company, because she's such a lonely little girl, always going off by herself. And she'll love looking after you all. Only you'll have to be careful not to disturb your Uncle Quentin. He's working very hard, and he isn't very good-tempered when he's disturbed.'

'We'll be as quiet as mice in the house!' said Dick. 'When are we going, Dad?'

'Next week, if that's all right with Mum,' said Dad.

Mum nodded. 'Yes,' she said, 'there's nothing much to get ready for them – just swimming costumes and jumpers and jeans. They all wear the same.'

'It'll be lovely to wear jeans again,' said Anne, dancing around. 'I'm sick of wearing my school uniform. I want to wear jeans, or a swimming costume, and go swimming and climbing.'

'Well, you'll soon be doing it,' said Mum, with a laugh. 'Remember to put ready any toys or books you want, won't you? Not many, please, because there won't be a lot of room.'

'Anne wanted to take all her fifteen teddies with her last year,' said Dick. 'Do you remember, Anne? That was funny!'

'No it wasn't,' said Anne, going red. 'I love my bears, and I just couldn't choose which to take – so I thought I'd take them all. There's nothing funny about that.'

'And do you remember the year before, Anne wanted to take the rocking-horse?' said Dick, with a giggle.

Mum chimed in. 'You know, I remember a little

boy called Dick who put aside one teddy bear, three toy dogs, two toy cats and his old monkey to take down to Polseath one year,' she said.

It was Dick's turn to go red. He changed the subject at once.

'Dad, are we going by train or by car?' he asked.

'By car,' said Dad. 'We can pile everything into the boot. Well – what about Tuesday?'

'That would suit me,' said Mum. 'We could take the children down, come back, and have plenty of time to do our own packing, and set off for Scotland on the Friday. Yes – we'll arrange for Tuesday.'

So Tuesday it was. The children counted the days eagerly, and Anne marked one off the calendar each night. The week seemed to pass very slowly. But at last Tuesday did come. Dick and Julian, who shared a room, woke up at about the same moment, and stared out of the nearby window.

'It's a lovely day!' cried Julian, leaping out of bed. 'I don't know why, but it always seems very important that it should be sunny on the first day of a holiday. Let's wake Anne.'

Anne slept in the next room. Julian ran in and shook her. 'Wake up! It's Tuesday! And the sun's shining.'

Anne woke up with a start and smiled at Julian happily. 'It's come at last!' she said. 'I thought it never would. Isn't it an exciting feeling to go away on holiday!'

They set off soon after breakfast. Their car was big, so it held them all very comfortably. Mum sat in front with Dad, and the three children sat behind, their feet on two suitcases. In the boot were all kinds of odds and ends, and one small trunk. Mum was sure they had remembered everything.

Along the crowded London roads they went, slowly at first, and then, as they left the town behind, more quickly. Soon they were right into the open country, and the car sped along fast. The children sang songs, as they always did when they were happy.

'Are we picnicking soon?' asked Anne, feeling hungry all of a sudden.

'Not yet,' said Mum. 'It's only eleven o'clock. We won't have lunch till at least half-past twelve, Anne.'

'Oh, Mum!' said Anne. 'I can't hold out till then!'

Mum handed her some chocolate, and she and the boys munched happily, watching the hills, woods and fields as the car sped by.

The picnic was lovely. They had it on the top of a hill, in a sloping field that looked down into a sunny valley. Anne didn't really like a big brown cow which came up close and stared at her, but it went away when Dad told it to. The children ate ravenously, and Mum said that instead of having a picnic tea at half-past four they would have to go to a cafe somewhere, because they had eaten all the tea sandwiches as well as the lunch ones!

'What time will we reach Aunt Fanny's?' asked Julian, finishing the very last sandwich and wishing there were more.

'About six o'clock with luck,' said Dad. 'Now who wants to stretch their legs a bit? We've another long drive in the car, you know.'

The car seemed to eat up the miles as it purred along. Tea-time came, and then the three children began to feel excited all over again.

'We should watch out for the sea,' said Dick. 'I can smell it somewhere near!'

He was right. The car suddenly topped a hill – and there was the shining blue sea, calm and smooth in the evening sun. The three children gave a yell.

'There it is!'

'Isn't it gorgeous!'

'Oh, I want to swim this very minute!'

'Only twenty minutes now, before we're at Kirrin Bay,' said Dad. 'We've made good time. You'll see the bay soon – it's quite a big one – with a funny sort of island at the entrance of the bay.'

The children looked out for it as they drove along the coast. Then Julian gave a shout.

'There it is – that must be Kirrin Bay. Look, Dick – isn't it lovely and blue?'

'And look at the rocky little island guarding the entrance of the bay,' said Dick. 'I'd like to visit that.'

'Well, I'm sure you will,' said Mum. 'Now, let's look out for Aunt Fanny's house. It's called Kirrin Cottage.'

They soon found it. It stood on the low cliff overlooking the bay, and was a very old house indeed. It wasn't really a cottage, but quite a big house, built of old white stone. Roses climbed over the front of it, and the garden was full of flowers.

'Here's Kirrin Cottage,' said Dad, and he stopped the car in front of it. 'It's supposed to be about three hundred years old! Now – where's Quentin? Ah, there's Fanny!'

2 The strange cousin

The children's aunt had been watching for the car. She came running out of the old wooden door as soon as she saw it draw up outside. The children liked the look of her at once.

'Welcome to Kirrin!' she cried. 'Hello, all of you! It's lovely to see you!'

There were kisses all round, and then the children went into the house. They liked it. It felt old and a bit mysterious, and the furniture was old and very beautiful.

'Where's Georgina?' asked Anne, looking round for her unknown cousin.

'Oh, the naughty girl! I told her to wait in the garden for you,' said her aunt. 'Now she's gone off somewhere. I must tell you, children, you may find George a bit difficult at first – she's always been one on her own, you know, and at first may not like you being here. But you mustn't take any notice of that – she'll be all right in a short time.

I was very glad for George's sake that you were able to come. She badly needs other children to play with.'

'Do you call her "George"?' asked Anne, in surprise. 'I thought her name was Georgina.'

'So it is,' said her aunt. 'But George hates being a girl, and we have to call her George, as if she were a boy. The naughty girl won't answer if we call her Georgina.'

The children thought that Georgina sounded interesting. They wished she would come. But she didn't. Their Uncle Quentin suddenly appeared instead. He was a most extraordinary looking man, very tall, very dark, and with a rather fierce frown on his wide forehead.

'Hallo, Quentin!' said Dad. 'It's ages since I've seen you. I hope these three won't disturb you very much in your work.'

'Quentin is working on a very difficult book,' said Aunt Fanny. 'But he has a room all to himself on the other side of the house. So I don't expect he will be disturbed.'

Their uncle looked at the three children, and nodded to them. The frown didn't come off his face, and they all felt a little scared, and were glad that he worked in another part of the house.

'Where's George?' he said, in a deep voice.

'Gone off somewhere again,' said Aunt Fanny, sounding annoyed. 'I told her to stay here and meet her cousins.'

'She wants a good talking to,' said Uncle Quentin. The children couldn't quite make out whether he was joking or not. 'Well, children, I hope you have a good time here, and maybe you'll knock a little common-sense into George!'

There was no room at Kirrin Cottage for Mum and Dad to stay the night, so after a hurried supper they left to stay at a hotel in the nearest town. They planned to drive back to London immediately after breakfast the next day, so they said goodbye to the children that night.

Georgina still hadn't appeared. 'I'm sorry we haven't seen Georgina,' said Mum. 'Just give her our love and tell her we hope she'll enjoy playing with Dick, Julian and Anne.'

Then Mum and Dad went. The children felt a bit lonely as they watched the family car disappear round the corner of the road, but Aunt Fanny took them upstairs to show them their bedrooms, and they soon forgot to be sad.

The two boys were to sleep together in a room with slanting ceilings at the top of the house. It had a marvellous view of the bay. The boys were really delighted with it. Anne was to sleep with Georgina in a smaller room, whose windows looked over the moors at the back of the house. But one side-window looked over the sea, which pleased Anne very much. It was a nice room, and red roses nodded their heads in at the window.

'I do wish Georgina would come,' Anne said to her aunt. 'I want to see what she's like.'

'Well, she's a funny girl,' said her aunt. 'She can be very rude and haughty – but she's kind at heart, very loyal and absolutely truthful. Once she makes friends with you, she'll always be your friend – but she finds it very difficult indeed to make friends, which is a shame.'

Anne suddenly yawned. The boys frowned at her, because they knew what would happen next. And it did!

'Poor Anne! How tired you are! You must all go to bed straight away, and have a good night's sleep. Then you will wake up quite fresh tomorrow,' said Aunt Fanny.

'Anne, you *are* an idiot,' said Dick, crossly,

when his aunt had gone out of the room. 'You know what grown-ups think as soon as we yawn. I wanted to go down to the beach for a while.'

'I'm so sorry,' said Anne. 'Somehow I couldn't help it. And anyway, *you're* yawning now, Dick – and Julian too!'

So they were. They were really sleepy after their long drive. Secretly all of them longed to cuddle down into bed and shut their eyes.

'I wonder where Georgina is,' said Anne, as she said goodnight to the boys, and went to her own room. 'Isn't she odd – not waiting to welcome us – and not coming in for supper – and not even in yet! After all, she's sleeping in my room – goodness knows what time she'll be in!'

All three children were fast asleep before Georgina came up to bed! They didn't hear her open Anne's door. They didn't hear her get undressed and clean her teeth. They didn't hear the creak of her bed as she got into it. They were so tired that they heard nothing at all until the sun woke them in the morning.

When Anne woke up she couldn't think where she was at first. She lay in her little bed and looked up at the slanting ceiling, and at the red roses that nodded at the open window – and suddenly remembered.

'I'm at Kirrin Bay – and it's the holidays!' she said to herself, and wriggled her legs with happiness.

Then she looked across at the other bed. Someone was curled up under the bedclothes. Anne could just see the top of a curly head, and that was all. When the figure stirred a little, Anne spoke.

'I say! Are you Georgina?'

The girl in the opposite bed sat up and looked across at Anne. She had very short curly hair. Her face was tanned, and her very blue eyes looked as bright as forget-me-nots in her face. But her mouth was rather sulky, and she had a frown like her father's.

'No,' she said. 'I'm not Georgina.'

'Oh!' said Anne, in surprise. 'Then who are you?'

'I'm George,' said the girl. 'I shall only answer if you call me George. I hate being a girl. I won't be. I don't like doing the things that girls do. I like doing the things that boys do. I can climb better than any boy, and swim faster too. I can sail a boat as well as any fisherman on this coast. Call me George. Then I'll speak to you. But I won't if you don't.'

'Oh!' said Anne, thinking that her new cousin was extraordinary. 'All right! I don't care what I call you. George is a nice name, I think. I don't much like Georgina. Anyway, you look like a boy.'

'Do I really?' said George, the frown leaving her face for a moment. 'Mum was furious with me when I cut my hair short. I had hair all round my neck before; it was awful.'

The two girls stared at one another for a moment. 'Don't you hate being a girl?' asked George.

'No, of course not,' said Anne. 'You see – I like pretty dresses – and I love my soft toys.'

'Who cares about pretty dresses?' said George, in a scornful voice. 'And toys! Well, you *are* a baby, that's all I can say.'

Anne felt offended. 'You're not very polite,' she said. 'My brothers won't take much notice of you if you act as if you know everything. They're *real* boys, not pretend boys, like you.'

'Well, if they're nasty to me, I won't take any

notice of *them*,' said George, jumping out of bed. 'I didn't want any of you to come, anyway. Interfering with my life here! I'm quite happy on my own. Now I've got to put up with a silly girl who likes dresses and toys, and two stupid boy-cousins!'

Anne felt that they had made a very bad start. She said no more, but got dressed. She put on her old jeans and a red jumper. George put on jeans too, and a boy's jumper. Just as they were ready the boys hammered on their door.

'Are you up? Is Georgina there? Cousin Georgina, come out and see us.'

George flung open the door and marched out with her head high. She took no notice of the two surprised boys at all. She stalked downstairs. The other three children looked at one another.

'She won't answer if you call her Georgina,' explained Anne. 'She's very odd, I think. She says she didn't want us to come because we'll interfere with her life. She laughed at me, and she was really rude.'

Julian put his arm round Anne, who looked a bit unhappy. 'Cheer up!' he said. 'You've got us to stick up for you. Come on down to breakfast.'

They were all hungry. The smell of bacon and eggs was very good. They ran down the stairs and said good-morning to their aunt. She was just bringing the breakfast to the table. Their uncle was sitting at the head, reading his paper. He nodded at the children. They sat down without a word, wondering if they were allowed to speak at meals. They always were at home, but their Uncle Quentin looked incredibly fierce.

George was there, buttering a piece of toast. She scowled at the three children.

'Don't look like that, George,' said her mother. 'I hope you've made friends already. It will be fun for you to play together. You must take your cousins to see the bay this morning and show them the best places to swim.'

'I'm going fishing,' said George.

Her father looked up at once.

'You are not,' he said. 'You're going to show a few good manners for a change, and take your cousins to the bay. Do you hear me?'

'Yes,' said George, with a scowl exactly like her father's.

'Oh, we can go to the bay by ourselves, if George is going fishing,' said Anne, at once, thinking that it would be nice not to have George if she was in a bad mood.

'George will do exactly as she's told,' said her father. 'If she doesn't, I'll deal with her.'

So, after breakfast, four children got ready to go down to the beach. An easy path led down to the bay, and they ran down happily. Even George lost her frown as she felt the warmth of the sun and saw the dancing sparkles on the blue sea.

'You go fishing if you want to,' said Anne when they were down on the beach. 'We won't tell on you. We don't want to interfere with you, you know. We've got ourselves for company, and if you don't want to be with us, you don't have to.'

'But we'd like you, all the same, if you'd like to be with us,' said Julian, generously. He thought George was rude and bad-tempered, but he couldn't help liking the look of the straight-backed, short-haired little girl, with her brilliant blue eyes and sulky mouth.

George stared at him. 'I'll see,' she said. 'I don't make friends with people just because they're my cousins, or anything silly like that. I only make friends with people if I like them.'

'So do we,' said Julian. 'We may not like you, of course.'

'Oh!' said George, as if that thought hadn't occurred to her. 'Well – you may not, of course. Lots of people don't like me, now I come to think of it.'

Anne was staring out over the blue bay. At the entrance to it lay a rocky island with what looked like an old ruined castle on the top of it.

'Isn't that a funny place?' she said. 'I wonder what it's called.'

'It's called Kirrin Island,' said George, her eyes as blue as the sea as she turned to look at it. 'It's a lovely place. If I like you, I may take you there some day. But I don't promise. The only way to get there is by boat.'

'Who does the funny island belong to?' asked Julian.

George gave a very surprising answer. 'It belongs to *me*,' she said. 'At least, it *will* belong to me – some day! It will be my very own island – and my very own castle!'

3 A peculiar story – and a new friend

The three children stared at George in the greatest surprise.

George stared back at them.

'What do you mean?' said Dick, at last. 'Kirrin Island can't belong to you. You're just boasting.'

'No, I'm not,' said George. 'You ask Mum. If you're not going to believe what I say I won't tell you another thing. But I don't tell lies. I think it's cowardly not to tell the truth – and I'm not a coward.'

Julian remembered that Aunt Fanny had said that George was absolutely truthful, and he scratched his head and looked at George again. How could she be telling the truth?

'Well, of course we'll believe you if you tell us the truth,' he said. 'But it does sound a bit unlikely, you know. Children don't usually own islands, even funny little ones like that.'

'It *isn't* a funny little island,' said George, fiercely. 'It's lovely. There are rabbits there, as tame as can be – and the big cormorants sit on the other side – and all kinds of gulls go there. The castle is wonderful too, even if it is all in ruins.'

'It sounds brilliant,' said Dick. 'How come it belongs to you, Georgina?'

George glared at him and didn't answer.

'Sorry,' said Dick, hastily. 'I didn't mean to call you Georgina. I meant to call you George.'

'Go on, George – tell us how the island belongs to you,' said Julian, slipping his arm through his sulky little cousin's.

She pulled away from him at once.

'Don't do that,' she said. 'I'm not sure that I want to make friends with you yet.'

'Fine,' said Julian, losing patience. 'Be enemies or anything you like. We don't care. But we like your mum, and we don't want her to think we won't make friends with you.'

'Do you like my mum?' said George, her bright blue eyes softening a little. 'Yes – she's great, isn't she? Well – all right – I'll tell you how Kirrin Castle belongs to me. Come and sit down here in this corner where nobody can hear us.'

They all sat down in a sandy corner of the beach. George looked across at the little island in the bay.

'It's like this,' she said. 'Years ago Mum's family owned nearly all the land around here. Then they got poor, and had to sell most of it. But they could never sell that little island, because nobody thought it was worth anything, especially as the castle has been ruined for years.'

'Imagine nobody wanting to buy a little island like that!' said Dick. 'I'd buy it at once if I had the money.'

'All that's left of what Mum's family owned is our house, Kirrin Cottage, and a farm a little way off – and Kirrin Island,' said George. 'Mum says when I'm grown-up it'll be mine. She says she doesn't want it now, either, so she's sort of given it to me. It belongs to me. It's my own private island, and I don't let anyone go there unless they get my permission.'

The three children stared at her. They believed every word George said, for it was quite plain that she was telling the truth.

'Oh, Georgina – I mean George!' said Dick. 'You're so lucky. It looks like a really nice island.

I hope you'll be friends with us and take us there one day soon. You can't imagine how much we'd love it.'

'Well – I might,' said George, pleased at the interest she had caused. 'I'll see. I've never taken anyone there before, though some of the boys and girls round here have begged me to. But I don't like them, so I haven't.'

There was a little silence as the four children looked out over the bay to where the island lay in the distance. The tide was going out. It almost looked as if they could wade over to the island. Dick asked if it was possible.

'No,' said George. 'I told you – it's only possible to get to it by boat. It's farther out than it looks – and the water is very, very deep. There are rocks all around it too – you have to know exactly where to row a boat, or you bump into them. It's a dangerous bit of coast here. There are a lot of wrecks about.'

'Wrecks!' cried Julian, his eyes shining. 'I've never seen an old wreck. Are there any to see?'

'Not now,' said George. 'They've all been cleared up. Except one, and that's the other side of the island. It's deep down in the water. You can just see the broken mast if you row over it on a calm day and look down into the water. That wreck really belongs to me too.'

This time the children really could hardly believe George. But she nodded her head firmly.

'Yes,' she said, 'it was a ship belonging to one of my great-great-great-grandfathers, or someone like that. He was bringing gold – big bars of gold – back in his ship – and it got wrecked off Kirrin Island.'

'Oooh – what happened to the gold?' asked Anne, her eyes round and big.

'Nobody knows,' said George. 'I expect it was stolen out of the ship. Divers have been down to see, of course, but they couldn't find any gold.'

'This does sound exciting,' said Julian. 'I wish I could see the wreck.'

'Well – we might perhaps go this afternoon when the tide is right down,' said George. 'The water is so calm and clear today. We could see a bit of it.'

'Oh, how wonderful!' said Anne. 'I'd love to see a real live wreck!'

The others laughed. 'Well, it won't be very alive,' said Dick. 'George – how about a swim?'

'I must go and get Timothy first,' said George. She got up.

'Who's Timothy?' said Dick.

'Can you keep a secret?' asked George. 'Nobody must know at home.'

'Well, go on, what's the secret?' asked Julian. 'You can tell us. We're not sneaks.'

'Timothy is my very greatest friend,' said George. 'I couldn't do without him. But Mum and Dad don't like him, so I have to keep him in secret. I'll go and fetch him.'

She ran off up the cliff path. The others watched her go. They thought she was the most peculiar girl they had ever known.

'Who can Timothy be?' wondered Julian. 'Some local boy, I suppose, that George's parents don't approve of.'

The children lay back in the soft sand and waited. Soon they heard George's clear voice coming down from the cliff behind them.

'Come on, Timothy! Come on!'

They sat up and looked to see what Timothy was like. They saw no boy – but instead a big brown mongrel dog with an absurdly long tail and a big wide mouth that really seemed to grin!

He was bounding all round George, mad with delight. She came running down to them.

'This is Timothy,' she said. 'Isn't he perfect?'

As a dog, Timothy was far from perfect. He was the wrong shape, his head was too big, his ears were too pricked, his tail was too long and it was quite impossible to say what kind of a dog he was supposed to be. But he was such a mad, friendly, clumsy, laughable creature that every one of the children adored him at once.

'Oh, you darling!' said Anne, and got a lick on the nose.

'Isn't he brilliant!' said Dick, and gave Timothy a friendly smack that made the dog bound madly all round him.

'I wish I had a dog like this,' said Julian, who really loved dogs, and had always wanted one of his own. 'Oh, George – he's great. You must be really proud of him!'

The girl smiled, and her face altered at once, and became sunny and pretty. She sat down on the sand and her dog cuddled up to her, licking her wherever he could find a bare piece of skin.

'I love him to bits,' she said. 'I found him out on the moors when he was just a pup, a year ago, and I took him home. At first Mum liked him, but when he grew bigger he got terribly naughty.'

'What did he do?' asked Anne.

'Well, he's a chewy kind of dog,' said George. 'He chewed up everything he could – a new rug Mum had bought – her nicest shoes – Dad's slippers – some of his papers, and things like that. And he barked too. I liked his bark, but Dad didn't. He said it nearly drove him mad. He hit Timothy and that made me angry, so I was rude to him.'

'Did you get told off?' said Anne. 'I wouldn't like to be rude to your dad. He looks fierce.'

George looked out over the bay. Her face had gone sulky again. 'Well, it doesn't matter what punishment I got,' she said, 'but the worst part of all was when Dad said I couldn't keep Timothy any more, and Mum backed Dad up and said Tim must go. I cried for days – and I *never* cry, you know, because boys don't and I like to be like a boy.'

'Boys do cry sometimes,' began Anne, looking at Dick, who had been a bit of a cry-baby three or four years back. Dick gave her a sharp nudge, and she said no more.

George looked at Anne.

'Boys don't cry,' she said, obstinately. 'Anyway, I've never seen one, and I always try not to cry myself. It's so babyish. But I just couldn't help it when Timothy had to go. He cried too.'

The children looked with great respect at Timothy. They had not known that a dog could cry before.

'Do you mean – he cried real tears?' asked Anne.

'No, not quite,' said George. 'He's too brave for that. He cried with his voice – howled and howled and looked so miserable that he nearly broke my heart. And then I knew I couldn't possibly part with him.'

'What happened then?' asked Julian.

'I went to Alf, a fisherman's son I know,' said George, 'and I asked him if he'd keep Tim for me, if I paid him all the pocket-money I get. He said he would, and so he does. That's why I never have any money to spend – it all has to go on Tim. He seems to eat an awful lot – don't you, Tim?'

'Woof!' said Tim, and rolled over on his back, all his shaggy legs in the air. Julian tickled him.

'How do you manage when you want sweets or

ice-cream?' said Anne, who spent most of her pocket-money on things of that sort.

'I don't manage,' said George. 'I go without, of course.'

This sounded awful to the other children, who loved ice-cream, chocolate and sweets. They stared at George.

'Well – I suppose the other children who play on the beach share their sweets with you sometimes, don't they?' asked Julian.

'I don't let them,' said George. 'If I can never give them any myself it's not fair to take them. So I say no.'

The sound of an ice-cream van's bell was heard in the distance. Julian felt in his pocket. He jumped up and rushed off, jingling his money. In a few moments he was back again, carrying four fat chocolate ice-cream bars. He gave one to Dick, and one to Anne, and then held out one to George. She looked at it longingly, but shook her head.

'No, thanks,' she said. 'You know what I just said. I haven't any money to buy them, so I can't share mine with you, and I can't take any from you. It's mean to take from people if you can't give even a little back.'

'You can take from us,' said Julian, trying to put the ice into George's brown hand. 'We're your cousins.'

'No, thanks,' said George again. 'Though I do think it's nice of you.'

She looked at Julian out of her blue eyes and the boy frowned as he tried to think of a way to make the obstinate girl take the ice. Then he smiled.

'Listen,' he said, 'you've got something we badly want to share – in fact you've got a lot of things we'd like to share, if only you'd let us. You share those with us, and let us share things like ice-cream with you. OK?'

'What things have I got that you want to share?' asked George, in surprise.

'You've got a dog,' said Julian, patting the big brown mongrel. 'We'd love to share him with you, he's great. And you've got a lovely island. We'd be really excited if you'd share it sometimes. And you've got a wreck. We'd like to look at it and share it too. Ice-cream and sweets aren't as good as those things – but it'd be nice to make a bargain and share with each other.'

George looked at the brown eyes that gazed

steadily into hers. She couldn't help liking Julian. It wasn't her nature to share anything. She had always been a lonely, rather misunderstood girl, fierce and hot-tempered. She had never had any friends of her own. Timothy looked up at Julian and saw that he was offering something nice and chocolatey to George. He jumped up and licked the boy with his friendly tongue.

'There you are, you see – Tim wants to be shared,' said Julian, with a laugh. 'It'd be nice for him to have three new friends.'

'Yes – it would,' said George, giving in suddenly, and taking the chocolate ice-cream bar. 'Thanks, Julian. I will share with you. But promise you'll never tell anyone at home that I'm still keeping Timothy?'

'Of course we'll promise,' said Julian. 'But I don't think that your dad or mum would mind, so long as Tim doesn't live in the house. How's the ice-cream? Is it nice?'

'Ooooh – the best one I've ever tasted!' said George nibbling at it. 'It's so cold. I haven't had one this year. It's simply delicious!'

Timothy tried to nibble it too. George gave him a few crumbs at the end. Then she turned and

4 An exciting afternoon

They all had a swim that morning, and the boys found that George was a much better swimmer than they were. She was very strong and very fast, and she could swim under water, too, holding her breath for ages.

'You're really good,' said Julian, admiringly. 'It's a pity Anne isn't a bit better. Anne, you'll have to practise your swimming strokes hard, or you'll never be able to swim out as far as we do.'

They were all very hungry by lunch-time. They went back up the cliff path, hoping there would be lots to eat – and there was! Cold meat and salad, plum pie and custard, and cheese afterwards. They all tucked in eagerly!

'What are you going to do this afternoon?' asked George's mother.

'George is going to take us out in a boat to see the wreck on the other side of the island,' said Anne. Her aunt looked most surprised.

'*George* is going to take you!' she said. 'George – what's come over you? You've never taken a single person before, though I've asked you to dozens of times!'

George said nothing, but went on eating her plum pie. She hadn't said a word all through the meal. Her father had not appeared at the table, much to the children's relief.

'Well, George, I must say I'm pleased that you want to try and do what your father said,' began her mother again. But George shook her head.

'I'm not doing it because I've got to,' she said. 'I'm doing it because I want to. I wouldn't have taken anyone to see my wreck, not even the King of England, if I didn't like them.'

Her mother laughed. 'Well, it's good news that you like your cousins,' she said. 'I hope they like you!'

'Oh yes!' said Anne, eagerly, anxious to stick up for her strange cousin. 'We do like George – and we like Ti—'

She was just about to say that they liked Timothy too, when she got such a kick on her ankle that she cried out in pain and the tears came into her eyes. George glared at her.

'George! Why did you kick Anne like that when she was saying nice things about you?' cried her mother. 'Leave the table at once. I won't have such behaviour.'

George left the table without a word. She went out into the garden. She had just taken a piece of bread and cut herself some cheese. It was all left on her plate. The other three stared at it in distress. Anne was upset. How could she have been so silly as to forget she mustn't mention Tim?

'Oh, please call George back!' she said. 'She didn't mean to kick me. It was an accident.'

But her aunt was very angry with George. 'Finish your meal,' she said to the others. 'I expect George will go into a sulk now. She is such a difficult girl!'

The others didn't mind about George going into a sulk. What they did mind was that George might refuse to take them to see the wreck now!

They finished the meal in silence. Their aunt went to see if Uncle Quentin wanted any more pie. He was having his meal in the study by himself. As soon as she had gone out of the room, Anne picked up the bread and cheese from George's plate and went out into the garden.

The boys didn't tell her off. They knew that Anne's tongue very often ran away with her – but she always tried to make up for it afterwards. They thought it was very brave of her to go and find George.

George was lying on her back under a big tree in the garden. Anne went up to her. 'I'm sorry I nearly made a mistake, George,' she said. 'Here's your bread and cheese. I've brought it for you. I promise I'll never forget not to mention Tim again.'

George sat up. 'I've a good mind not to take you to see the wreck,' she said. 'Stupid baby!'

Anne's heart sank. This was what she had feared. 'Well,' she said, 'you needn't take me, of course. But you could take the boys, George. After all, they didn't do anything silly. And anyway, you gave me an awful kick. Look at the bruise.'

George looked at it. Then she looked at Anne. 'But wouldn't you be miserable if I took Julian and Dick without you?' she asked.

'Of course,' said Anne. 'But I don't want to make them miss a treat, even if I have to.'

Then George did a surprising thing for her. She

gave Anne a hug! Then she immediately looked most ashamed of herself, for she felt sure that no boy would have done that! And she always tried to act like a boy.

'It's all right,' she said, gruffly, taking the bread and cheese. 'You were nearly very silly – and I gave you a kick – so we're even. Of course you can come this afternoon.'

Anne sped back to tell the boys that everything was all right – and in fifteen minutes' time four children ran down to the beach. By a boat was a brown-faced boy, about fourteen years old. He had Timothy with him.

'Boat's all ready, George,' he said with a grin. 'And Tim's ready, too.'

'Thanks, Alf,' said George, and told the others to get in. Timothy jumped in, too, his big tail wagging nineteen to the dozen. George pushed the boat off into the surf and then jumped in herself. She took the oars.

She rowed very well, and the boat shot along over the blue bay. It was a wonderful afternoon, and the children loved the movement of the boat over the water. Timothy stood at the prow and barked whenever a wave reared its head.

'He's funny on a wild day,' said George, pulling hard. 'He barks madly at the big waves, and gets so angry if they splash him. He's a really good swimmer.'

'Isn't it nice to have a dog with us?' said Anne, anxious to make up for her mistake. 'I do so like him.'

'Woof,' said Timothy, in his deep voice and turned round to lick Anne's ear.

'I'm sure he knew what I said,' said Anne in delight.

'Of course he did,' said George. 'He understands every single word.'

'We're getting near to your island now,' said Julian, in excitement. 'It's bigger than I thought. And isn't the castle exciting?'

They drew near to the island, and the children saw that there were sharp rocks all around it. Unless anyone knew exactly the way to take, no boat or ship could possibly land on the shore of the rocky little island. In the very middle of it, on a low hill, rose the ruined castle. It had been built of big white stones. Broken archways, tumbledown towers, ruined walls – that was all that was left of a once beautiful castle, proud and strong. Now the jackdaws nested in it and the gulls sat on the topmost stones.

'It looks so mysterious,' said Julian. 'I'd love to land there and have a look at the castle. Wouldn't it be fun to spend a night or two here!'

George stopped rowing. Her face lit up. 'Yes!' she said, in delight. 'Do you know, I never thought how lovely that would be! To spend a night on my island! To be there all alone, the four of us. To get our own meals, and pretend we really lived there. Wouldn't it be brilliant?'

'Amazing,' agreed Dick, looking longingly at the island. 'Do you think your mum would let us?'

'I don't know,' said George. 'She might. You could ask her.'

'Can't we land there this afternoon?' asked Julian.

'No, not if you want to see the wreck,' said George. 'We've got to get back for tea today, and it will take all the time to row round to the other side of Kirrin Island and back.'

'Well – I'd like to see the wreck,' said Julian, torn between the island and the wreck. 'Here, let me take the oars for a bit, George. You can't do all the rowing.'

'I can,' said George. 'But I'd quite enjoy lying back in the boat for a change! Look – I'll just take you by this rocky bit – and then you can take the oars till we come to another awkward piece. The rocks around this bay are dreadful!'

George and Julian changed places in the boat. Julian rowed well, but not as strongly as George. The boat sped along rocking smoothly. They went right round the island, and saw the castle from the other side. It looked more ruined on the side that faced the sea.

'The strong winds come from the open sea,' explained George. 'There's not really much left of it this side, except piles of stones. But there's a good little harbour in a small cove, if you know how to find it.'

George took the oars after a while, and rowed steadily out a little beyond the island. Then she stopped and looked back towards the shore.

'How do you know when you're over the wreck?' asked Julian, puzzled. 'I'd never know!'

'See that church tower on the mainland?' asked George. 'And the tip of that hill over there? Well, when you get them exactly in line with one another, between the two towers of the castle on the island, you're pretty much over the wreck! I found that out ages ago.'

The children saw that the tip of the far-off hill and the church tower were almost in line, when they looked at them between the two old towers of the island castle. They looked eagerly down into the sea to see if they could spot the wreck.

The water was perfectly clear and smooth. There was hardly a ripple. Timothy looked down into it too, his head on one side, his ears cocked, just as if he knew what he was looking for! The children laughed at him.

'We're not exactly over it,' said George, looking down too. 'The water's so clear today that we should be able to see quite a long way down. Wait, I'll row a bit to the left.'

'Woof!' said Timothy, suddenly, and wagged his tail – and at the same moment the three children saw something deep down in the water!

'It's the wreck!' said Julian, almost falling out of the boat in his excitement. 'I can see a bit of broken mast. Look, Dick, look!'

All four children and the dog, too, gazed down earnestly into the clear water. After a little while they could make out the outlines of a dark hulk, out of which the broken mast stood.

'It's a bit on one side,' said Julian. 'Poor old ship. It must hate lying there, slowly falling to pieces. George, I wish I could dive down and get a closer look at it.'

'Well, why don't you?' said George. 'You've got your swimming trunks on. I've often dived down. I'll come with you, if you like, if Dick can keep the boat round about here. There's a current that's trying to take it out to sea. Dick, you'll have to keep working a bit with this oar to keep the boat in one spot.'

The girl stripped off her jeans and jumper and Julian did the same. George had on a swimming costume underneath and Julian had on his swimming trunks. George did a beautiful dive off the end of the boat, deep down into the water. The others watched her swimming strongly downwards, holding her breath.

After a bit she came up, almost bursting for breath. 'Well, I went almost down to the wreck,' she said. 'It's just the same as it always is – seaweedy and covered with limpets and things. I wish I could get right into the ship itself. But I never have enough breath for that. You go down now, Julian.'

So down Julian went – but he wasn't as good at swimming deep under water as George was, and he couldn't go down as far. He knew how to open his eyes under water, so he was able to take a good look at the deck of the wreck. It looked very abandoned and strange. Julian didn't really like it very much. It gave him a sad sort of feeling. He was glad to go to the surface again, and take deep breaths of air, and feel the warm sunshine on his shoulders.

He climbed into the boat. 'That was really exciting,' he said. 'I'd love to see that wreck properly – you know – go down under the deck into the cabins and look around. Imagine if we could really find the boxes of gold!'

'That's impossible,' said George. 'I told you proper divers have already gone down and found nothing. What's the time? We'll be late if we don't hurry back now!'

They did hurry back, and managed to be only about five minutes late for tea. Afterwards they went for a walk over the moors, with Timothy at their heels, and by the time that bedtime came they were all so sleepy that they could hardly keep their eyes open.

'Goodnight, George,' said Anne, snuggling down into her bed. 'We've had a lovely day – thanks to you!'

'And *I've* had a lovely day, too,' said George, rather gruffly. 'Thanks to *you*. I'm glad you all came. We're going to have fun. And you'll love my castle and my little island!'

'Oooh, yes,' said Anne, and fell asleep to dream of wrecks and castles and islands by the hundred. When would George take them to her little island?

5 A visit to the island

The children's aunt arranged a picnic for them the next day, and they all went off to a little cove not far away where they could swim and paddle to their hearts' content. They had a wonderful day, but secretly Julian, Dick and Anne wished they could have visited George's island. They would rather have done that than anything!

George didn't want to go for the picnic, not because she disliked picnics, but because she couldn't take her dog. Her mother went with them, and George had to spend a whole day without her beloved Timothy.

'Bad luck!' said Julian, who guessed what she was unhappy about. 'I think you should tell your mum about Tim. I'm sure she wouldn't mind you letting someone else keep him for you. I know my mum wouldn't mind.'

'I'm not going to tell anybody but you,' said George. 'I'm always getting into trouble at home.

It's probably my own fault, but I get a bit tired of it. You see, Dad doesn't make much money with the books he writes, and he's always wanting to give Mum and me things he can't afford. So that makes him bad-tempered. He wants to send me away to a good school but he hasn't got the money. I'm glad. I don't want to go away to school. I like being here. I couldn't bear to part with Timothy.'

'You'd like boarding school,' said Anne. 'We all go. It's fun.'

'No, it isn't,' said George obstinately. 'It must be awful to be one of a crowd, and to have other girls all laughing and yelling round you. I'd hate it.'

'No, you wouldn't,' said Anne. 'All that is great fun. I think it'd be good for you, George.'

'Don't start telling me what's good for me,' said George, suddenly looking very fierce. 'Mum and Dad are always saying that things are good for me – and they are always the things I don't like.'

'All right, all right,' said Julian, beginning to laugh. 'No need to flare up like that! Honestly, I think we could light a fire from the sparks that fly from your eyes!'

That made George laugh, though she didn't want to. It was really impossible to sulk with Julian around.

They went off to swim in the sea for the fifth time that day. Soon they were all splashing about happily, and George helped Anne to swim better. The younger girl hadn't got the right stroke, and George felt really proud when she had taught her.

'Oh, thanks,' said Anne, struggling along. 'I'll never be as good as you – but I'd like to be as good as the boys.'

As they were going home, George spoke to Julian. 'Could you say that you want to go and buy a stamp or something?' she said. 'Then I could go with you, and just look in on Tim. He'll be wondering why I haven't taken him out today.'

'Sure!' said Julian. 'I don't want stamps, but I *could* do with an ice-cream. Dick and Anne can go home with your mum and carry the things. I'll just go and tell Aunt Fanny.'

He ran up to his aunt. 'Do you mind if I go and buy some ice-creams?' he asked. 'We haven't had one today. I won't be long. Can George go with me?'

'I don't expect she will want to,' said his aunt. 'But you can ask her.'

'George, come with me!' yelled Julian, setting off to the little village at a great pace. George gave a sudden grin and ran after him. She soon caught him up and smiled gratefully at him.

'Thanks,' she said. 'You go and get the ice-creams, and I'll go and see Tim.'

They parted, Julian bought four ice-creams, and turned to go home. He waited about for George, who came running up after a few minutes. Her face was glowing.

'He's all right,' she said. 'He was really pleased to see me! He nearly jumped over my head. Oh – another ice-cream for me! Thanks so much, Julian. I'll have to share something with you quickly. What about going to my island tomorrow?'

'Yes!' said Julian, his eyes shining. 'That'd be brilliant. Come on, let's tell the others!'

The four children sat in the garden eating their ice-creams. Julian told them what George had said. They all felt excited. George was pleased. She had always felt quite important before when she had refused to take any of the other children to see Kirrin Island – but it felt much nicer somehow to have agreed to row her cousins there.

'I used to think it was much, much nicer always to do things on my own,' she thought, as she sucked the last bits of her ice-cream. 'But it's going to be fun doing things with Julian and the others.'

The children were sent to wash themselves and to get tidy before supper. They talked eagerly about the visit to the island next day. Their aunt heard them and smiled.

'Well, I really must say I'm pleased that George is going to share something with you,' she said. 'Would you like to take your dinner there, and spend the day? It's hardly worthwhile rowing all the way there and landing unless you're going to spend some hours there.'

'Oh, Aunt Fanny! That'd be great!' cried Anne.

George looked up. 'Are you coming too, Mum?' she asked.

'You don't sound at all as if you want me to,' said her mother, in a hurt tone. 'You looked cross yesterday, too, when you found I was coming. No – I won't come tomorrow – but I'm sure your cousins must think you're an odd girl never to want your mother to go with you.'

George said nothing. She hardly ever did say a word when she was told off. The others said nothing too. They knew perfectly well that it wasn't that George didn't want her mother to go – it was just that she wanted Timothy with her!

'Anyway, I couldn't come,' went on Aunt Fanny. 'I've some gardening to do. You'll be quite safe with George. She can handle a boat like a grown-up.'

The three children looked eagerly at the weather the next day when they got up. The sun was shining, and everything seemed splendid.

'Isn't it a gorgeous day?' said Anne to George, as they dressed. 'I'm so looking forward to going to the island.'

'I'm not sure we should go after all,' said George, unexpectedly.

'Oh, but why?' cried Anne, in dismay.

'I think there's going to be a storm or something,' said George, looking out to the south-west.

'But, George, why do you say that?' said Anne, impatiently. 'Look at the sun – and there's hardly a cloud in the sky!'

'The wind is wrong,' said George. 'And can't

you see the little white tops of the waves out there by my island? That's always a bad sign.'

'Oh, George – it will be the biggest disappointment of our lives if we don't go today,' said Anne, who couldn't bear any disappointment, big or small. 'And besides,' she added, craftily, 'if we hang about the house, afraid of a storm, we won't be able to have Tim with us.'

'Yes, that's true,' said George. 'All right – we'll go. But mind – if a storm does come, you're not to be a baby. You're to try and enjoy it and not be frightened.'

'Well, I don't much like storms,' began Anne, but stopped when she saw George's scornful look. They went down to breakfast, and George asked her mother if they could take their dinner as they had planned.

'Yes,' said her mother. 'You and Anne can help to make the sandwiches. You boys can go into the garden and pick some ripe plums to take with you. Julian, you can go down to the village when you've done that and buy some bottles of lemonade or ginger-beer, whichever you like.'

'Ginger-beer for me, thanks!' said Julian, and everyone else said the same. They all felt very happy. It would be exciting to visit the strange little island. George felt happy because she would be with Tim all day.

They set off at last, the food in two rucksacks. The first thing they did was to fetch Tim. He was tied up in Alf's back garden. Alf himself was there, and grinned at George.

'Morning, George,' he said. 'Tim's been barking his head off for you. I guess he knew you were coming for him today.'

'Of course he did,' said George, untying him. He at once went completely mad, and tore round and round the children, his tail down and his ears flat.

'He'd win any race if only he were a greyhound,' said Julian, admiringly. 'You can hardly see him for dust. Tim! Hey, Tim! Come and say "Good-morning".'

Tim leapt up and licked Julian's left ear as he passed on his whirlwind way. Then he sobered down and ran lovingly by George as they all made their way to the beach. He licked George's bare legs every now and again, and she pulled at his ears gently.

They got into the boat, and George pushed off.

Alf waved to them. 'You won't be very long, will you?' he called. 'There's a storm blowing up. Bad one it'll be, too.'

'I know,' shouted back George. 'But maybe we'll get back before it begins. It's pretty far off yet.'

George rowed all the way to the island. Tim stood at each end of the boat in turn, barking when the waves reared up at him. The children watched the island coming closer and closer. It looked even more exciting than it had the other day.

'George, where are you going to land?' asked Julian. 'I don't know how you find your way in and out of these rocks. I'm afraid every moment we'll bump into them!'

'I'm going to land at the little cove I told you about the other day,' said George. 'There's only one way to it, but I know it very well. It's hidden away on the east side of the island.'

The girl cleverly worked her boat in and out of the rocks, and suddenly, as it rounded a low wall of sharp rocks, the others saw the cove she had spoken of. It was like a natural little harbour, and was a smooth inlet of water running up to a stretch of sand, sheltered between high rocks. The boat slid into the inlet, and at once stopped rocking, for here the water was like glass, and had hardly a ripple.

'This is brilliant!' said Julian, his eyes shining with delight. George looked at him and her eyes shone too, as bright as the sea itself. It was the first time she had ever taken anyone to her precious island, and she was enjoying it.

They landed on the smooth yellow sand. 'We're really on the island!' said Anne, and she capered about, Tim joining her and looking as mad as she did. The others laughed. George pulled the boat high up on the sand.

'Why so far up?' said Julian, helping her. 'The tide's almost in, isn't it? Surely it won't come as high as this.'

'I told you I thought a storm was coming,' said George. 'If one does, the waves simply tear up this inlet and we don't want to lose our boat, do we?'

'Let's explore the island, let's explore the island!' yelled Anne, who was now at the top of the little natural harbour, climbing up the rocks there. 'Come on!'

They all followed her. It was a very exciting place. Rabbits were everywhere! They scuttled about as the children appeared, but did not go into their holes.

'Aren't they tame!' said Julian, in surprise.

'Well, nobody ever comes here but me,' said George, 'and I don't frighten them. Tim! Tim, if you go after the rabbits, I'll be furious.'

Tim turned big sorrowful eyes on to George. He and George agreed about every single thing except rabbits. To Tim rabbits were made for one thing – to chase! He never could understand why George wouldn't let him do this. But he held himself in and walked solemnly by the children, his eyes watching the lolloping rabbits longingly.

'I believe they would almost eat out of my hand,' said Julian.

But George shook her head.

'No, I've tried that with them,' she said. 'They won't. Look at those baby ones. Aren't they lovely?'

'Woof!' said Tim, agreeing, and he took a few steps towards them. George made a warning noise in her throat, and Tim walked back, his tail down.

'There's the castle!' said Julian. 'Shall we explore that now? I really want to.'

'Yes, we will,' said George. 'Look – that's where the entrance used to be – through that big broken archway.'

The children gazed at the enormous old archway, now half broken down. Behind it were ruined stone steps leading towards the centre of the castle.

'It had strong walls all round it, with two towers,' said George. 'One tower is almost gone, as you can see, but the other isn't so bad. The jackdaws build in that every year. They've almost filled it up with their sticks!'

As they came near to the better tower of the two the jackdaws circled round them with loud cries of 'Chack, chack, chack!' Tim leapt into the air as if he thought he could get them, but they only called mockingly to him.

'This is the centre of the castle,' said George, as they entered through a ruined doorway into what looked like a great yard, whose stone floor was now overgrown with grass and other weeds. 'Here's where the people used to live. You can see where the rooms were – look, there's one almost whole there. Go through that little door and you'll see it.'

They trooped through a doorway and found themselves in a dark, stone-walled, stone-roofed room, with a space at one end where a fireplace must have been. Two slit-like windows lit the room. It felt very strange and mysterious.

'What a pity it's all broken down,' said Julian, wandering out again. 'That room seems to be the only one quite whole. There are some others here – but all of them seem to have either no roof, or one or other of the walls gone. That room is the only liveable one. Was there an upstairs to the castle, George?'

'Of course,' said George. 'But the steps that led up are gone. Look! You can see part of an upstairs room there, by the jackdaw tower. You can't get up to it, though, because I've tried. I nearly broke my neck trying to get up. The stones just crumble away.'

'Were there any dungeons?' asked Dick.

'I don't know,' said George. 'I expect so. But nobody could find them now – everywhere is so overgrown.'

It was indeed overgrown. Big blackberry bushes

grew here and there, and a few gorse bushes forced their way into gaps and corners. The coarse green grass sprang everywhere, and pink thrift grew its cushions in holes and crannies.

'Well, I think it's a lovely place,' said Anne. 'Completely and absolutely lovely!'

'Do you really?' said George, pleased. 'I'm so glad. Look! We're right on the other side of the island now, facing the sea. Do you see those rocks, with those big birds sitting there?'

The children looked. They saw some rocks sticking up, with great black shining birds sitting on them in strange positions.

'They are cormorants,' said George. 'They've caught plenty of fish for their dinner, and they're sitting there digesting it. Oh – they're all flying away. I wonder why?'

She soon knew – for, from the south-west there suddenly came an ominous rumble.

'Thunder!' said George. 'That's the storm. It's coming sooner than I thought!'

6 *What the storm did*

The four children stared out to sea. They had all been so interested in exploring the exciting old castle that not one of them had noticed the sudden change in the weather.

Another rumble came. It sounded like a big dog growling in the sky. Tim heard it and growled back, sounding like a small roll of thunder himself.

'We're in for it now,' said George, half-alarmed. 'We can't get back in time; it's blowing up at top speed. Did you ever see such a change in the sky?'

The sky had been blue when they started. Now it was overcast, and the clouds seemed to hang very low indeed. They scudded along as if someone was chasing them – and the wind howled round in such a mournful way that Anne felt quite frightened.

'It's beginning to rain,' said Julian, feeling an

enormous drop spatter on his outstretched hand. 'We'd better shelter, hadn't we, George? We'll get wet through.'

'Yes, we will in a minute,' said George. 'Just look at these big waves coming! It really is going to be a storm. Oh – what a flash of lightning!'

The waves were certainly beginning to run very high indeed. It was amazing to see what a change had come over them. They swelled up, turned over as soon as they came to rocks, and then rushed up the beach of the island with a great roar.

'I think we'd better pull our boat up higher still,' said George suddenly. 'It's going to be a very bad storm indeed. Sometimes these sudden summer storms are worse than a winter one.'

She and Julian ran to the other side of the island where they had left the boat. It was a good thing they went, for great waves were already racing right up to it. The two children pulled the boat up almost to the top of the low cliff and George tied it to a stout gorse bush growing there.

By now the rain was absolutely pelting down, and George and Julian were soaked. 'I hope the others have had the sense to shelter in that room that has a roof and walls,' said George.

They were in there, looking rather cold and scared. It was very dark there, for the only light came through the two slits of windows and the small doorway.

'Could we light a fire to make things a bit more cheerful?' said Julian, looking round. 'I wonder where we can find some nice dry sticks?'

Almost as if they were answering the question a small crowd of jackdaws cried out wildly as they circled in the storm. 'Chack, chack, chack!'

'Of course! There are plenty of sticks on the ground below the tower!' cried Julian. 'You know – where the jackdaws nest. They've dropped lots of sticks there.'

He dashed out into the rain and ran to the tower. He picked up an armful of sticks and ran back.

'Good,' said George. 'We'll be able to make a nice fire with those. Anyone got any paper to start it – or matches?'

'I've got some matches,' said Julian. 'But nobody's got paper.'

'Yes,' said Anne, suddenly. 'The sandwiches are wrapped in paper. Let's undo them, and then we can use the paper for the fire.'

'Good idea,' said George. So they undid the sandwiches, and put them neatly on a broken stone, rubbing it clean first. Then they built up a fire, with the paper underneath and the sticks arranged criss-cross on top.

It was fun when they lit the paper. It flared up and the sticks at once caught fire, for they were very old and dry. Soon there was a fine crackling fire going and the little ruined room was lit by dancing flames. It was very dark outside now, for the clouds hung almost low enough to touch the top of the castle tower! And how they raced by! The wind sent them off to the north-east, roaring behind them with a noise like the sea itself.

'I've never, never heard the sea making such an awful noise,' said Anne. 'Never! It really sounds as if it's shouting at the top of its voice.'

What with the howling of the wind and the crashing of the great waves all round the little island, the children could hardly hear themselves speak! They had to shout at one another.

'Let's have our dinner!' yelled Dick, who was feeling terribly hungry as usual. 'We can't do anything much while this storm lasts.'

'Yes, let's,' said Anne, looking longingly at the ham sandwiches. 'It'll be fun to have a picnic round the fire in this dark old room. I wonder how long ago other people had a meal here? I wish I could see them.'

'Well, I don't,' said Dick, looking round half-scared as if he expected to see ghostly people walk in to share their picnic. 'It's a strange enough day without wanting things like that to happen.'

They all felt better when they were eating the sandwiches and drinking the ginger-beer. The fire flared up as more and more sticks caught, and gave out a welcome warmth, for now that the wind had got up so strongly, the day had become cold.

'We'll take it in turns to fetch sticks,' said George. But Anne didn't want to go alone. She was trying her best not to show that she was afraid of the storm – but it was more than she could do to go out of the cosy room into the rain and thunder by herself.

Tim didn't seem to like the storm either. He sat close by George, his ears cocked, and growled whenever the thunder rumbled. The children fed him with titbits and he ate them eagerly, for he was hungry too.

All the children had four biscuits each. 'I think I'll give all mine to Tim,' said George. 'I didn't bring him any of his own biscuits, and he seems so hungry.'

'No, don't do that,' said Julian. 'We'll each give him a biscuit – that'll be four for him – and we'll still have three left each. That'll be plenty for us.'

'You're really nice,' said George. 'Tim, aren't they nice?'

Tim licked everyone and made them laugh. Then he rolled over on his back and let Julian tickle him underneath.

The children fed the fire and finished their picnic. When it came to Julian's turn to get more sticks, he disappeared out of the room into the storm. He stood and looked around, the rain wetting his bare head.

The storm seemed to be right overhead now. The lightning flashed and the thunder crashed at the same moment. Julian wasn't afraid of storms, but he couldn't help feeling rather over-awed at this one. It was so magnificent. The lightning tore the sky in half almost every minute, and the thunder crashed so loudly that it sounded almost as if mountains were falling down all around!

The sea's voice could be heard as soon as the thunder stopped – and that was magnificent to hear too. The spray flew so high into the air that it wetted Julian as he stood in the centre of the ruined castle.

'I'm going to see what the waves are like,' thought the boy. 'If the spray flies right over me here, they must be absolutely enormous!'

He made his way out of the castle and climbed up on to part of the ruined wall that had once run all round the castle. He stood up there, looking out to the open sea. And what a sight met his eyes!

The waves were like great walls of grey-green! They dashed over the rocks that lay all around the island, and spray flew from them, gleaming white in the stormy sky. They rolled up to the island and dashed themselves against it with such force that Julian could feel the wall beneath his feet tremble with the shock.

The boy looked out to sea, marvelling at the really great sight he saw. For half a moment he wondered if the sea might come right over the island itself! Then he knew that couldn't happen, for it would have happened before. He stared at the great waves coming in – and then he saw something very strange.

There was something else out on the sea by the rocks, besides the waves – something dark, something big, something that seemed to lurch out of the waves and settle down again. What could it be?

'It can't be a ship,' said Julian to himself, his heart beginning to beat fast as he strained his eyes to see through the rain and the spray. 'And yet it looks more like a ship than anything else. I hope it isn't a ship. There wouldn't be anyone saved from it on this dreadful day!'

He stood and watched for a while. The dark shape heaved into sight again and then sank away once more. Julian decided to go and tell the others. He ran back to the firelit room.

'George! Dick! There's something strange out on the rocks beyond the island!' he shouted, at the top of his voice. 'It looks like a ship – and yet it can't possibly be. Come and see!'

The others stared at him in surprise, and jumped

to their feet. George hurriedly flung some more
sticks on the fire to keep it going, and then she
and the others quickly followed Julian out
into the rain.

The storm seemed to be passing over a little
now. The rain wasn't pelting down quite so
hard. The thunder was rolling a little farther off,
and the lightning did not flash so often. Julian led
the way to the wall on which he had climbed to
watch the sea.

Everyone climbed up to gaze out to sea. They
saw a great tumbled, heaving mass of grey-green
water, with waves rearing up everywhere. Their
tops broke over the rocks and they rushed up to
the island as if they would gobble it whole. Anne
slipped her arm through Julian's. She felt small
and scared.

'You're all right, Anne,' said Julian, loudly.
'Now just watch – you'll see something strange
in a minute.'

They all watched. At first they saw nothing, for
the waves reared up so high that they hid
everything a little way out. Then suddenly George
saw what Julian meant.

'You're right!' she shouted. 'It is a ship! Yes, it

is! Is it being wrecked? It's a big ship – not a sailing-boat, or fishing-boat!'

'Oh, is anyone in it?' wailed Anne.

The four children watched and Tim began to bark as he saw the strange dark shape lurching here and there in the enormous waves. The sea was bringing the ship nearer to shore.

'It'll be dashed on to those rocks,' said Julian, suddenly. 'Look – there it goes!'

As he spoke there came a tremendous crashing, splintering sound, and the dark shape of the ship settled down on to the sharp teeth of the dangerous rocks on the south-west side of the island. It stayed there, shifting only slightly as the big waves ran under it and lifted it a little.

'She's stuck there,' said Julian. 'She won't move now. The sea will soon be going down a bit, and then the ship will find herself held by those rocks.'

As he spoke, a ray of pale sunshine came wavering out between a gap in the thinning clouds. It was gone almost at once. 'Good!' said Dick, looking upwards. 'The sun will be out again soon. We can warm ourselves then and get dry – and maybe we can find out what that poor ship is. I hope there was nobody in it. I hope they've all taken the lifeboats and got safely to land.'

The clouds thinned out a little more. The wind stopped roaring and dropped to a steady breeze. The sun shone out again for a longer time, and the children felt its welcome warmth. They all stared at the ship on the rocks. The sun shone on it and lighted it up.

'There's something odd about it somehow,' said Julian, slowly. 'Something really odd. I've never seen a ship quite like it.'

George was staring at it with a strange look in her eyes. She turned to face the three children, and they were astonished to see the bright gleam in her blue eyes. The girl looked almost too excited to speak.

'What is it?' asked Julian, grabbing her hand.

'Julian – oh, Julian – it's my wreck!' she cried, in a high excited voice. 'Don't you see what's happened? The storm's lifted the ship up from the bottom of the sea, and lodged it on those rocks. It's my wreck!'

The others saw at once that she was right. It was the old wrecked ship! No wonder it looked strange. No wonder it looked so old and dark,

7 *Back to Kirrin Cottage*

The four children were so surprised and excited that for a minute or two they didn't say a word. They just stared at the dark hulk of the old wreck, imagining what they might find. Then Julian clutched George's arm and pressed it tightly.

'Isn't this wonderful?' he said. 'George, isn't it an amazing thing to happen?'

Still George said nothing, but stared at the wreck, all kinds of thoughts racing through her mind. Then she turned to Julian.

'I hope the wreck is still mine now it's thrown up like this!' she said. 'I don't know if wrecks belong to the King or anyone, like lost treasure does. But after all, the ship did belong to our family. Nobody bothered much about it when it was down under the sea – but do you think people will still let me have it for my own now it's thrown up?'

'Well, don't let's tell anyone!' said Dick.

'Don't be silly,' said George. 'One of the fishermen is sure to see it when his ship goes slipping out of the bay. The news will soon be out.'

'Well, then, we'd better explore it thoroughly ourselves before anyone else does!' said Dick, eagerly. 'No one knows about it yet. Only us. Can't we explore it as soon as the waves go down a bit?'

'We can't wade out to the rocks, if that's what you mean,' said George. 'We might get there by boat – but we couldn't risk it now, while the waves are so big. They won't go down today. The wind is still too strong.'

'Well, what about tomorrow morning, early?' said Julian. 'Before anyone has got to know about it? I bet if only we can get into the ship first, we can find anything there is to find!'

'Yes, I expect we could,' said George. 'I told you divers had been down and explored the ship as thoroughly as they could – but of course it's difficult to do that properly under water. We might find something they've missed. Oh, this is like a dream. I can't believe it's true that my old wreck has come up from the bottom of the sea like that!'

The sun was now properly out, and the children's wet clothes dried in its hot rays. They steamed in the sun, and even Tim's coat sent up a mist too. He didn't seem to like the wreck at all, and growled deeply at it.

'You are funny, Tim,' said George, patting him. 'It won't hurt you! What do you think it is?'

'He probably thinks it's a whale,' said Anne with a laugh. 'Oh, George – this is the most exciting day of my life! Can't we take the boat and see if we can get to the wreck?'

'No, we can't,' said George. 'I only wish we could. But it's impossible, Anne. For one thing, I don't think the wreck has quite settled down on the rocks yet, and maybe it won't till the tide has gone down. I can see it lifting a little still when an extra big wave comes. It'd be dangerous to go into it yet. And for another thing I don't want my boat smashed to bits on the rocks, and us thrown into that wild water! That's what would happen. We have to wait till tomorrow. It's a good idea to come early. I expect lots of grown-ups will think it's their business to explore it.'

The children watched the old wreck for a little longer and then went all round the island again.

It was certainly not very large, but it really was exciting, with its rocky little coast, its quiet inlet where their boat was, the ruined castle, the circling jackdaws, and the scampering rabbits everywhere.

'I do love it,' said Anne. 'I really do. It's just small enough to *feel* like an island. Most islands are too big to feel like islands. I mean, Britain is an island, but nobody living on it could possibly know that unless they were told. This island really *feels* like one because wherever you are you can see to the other side of it. I love it.'

George felt very happy. She had often been on her island before, but always alone except for Tim. She had always vowed that she would never take anyone there, because it would spoil her island for her. But it hadn't been spoilt. It had made it much nicer. For the first time George began to understand that sharing pleasures doubles their joy.

'We'll wait till the waves go down a bit then we'll go back home,' she said. 'I think there's some more rain coming, and we'll only get soaked through. We shan't be back till tea-time as it is, because we'll have a long pull against the out-going tide.'

All the children felt tired after the excitements of the morning. They said very little as they rowed home. Everyone took turns at rowing except Anne, who wasn't strong enough with the oars to row against the tide. They looked back at the island as they left it. They couldn't see the wreck because that was on the opposite side, facing the open sea.

'It's just as well it's there,' said Julian. 'No one can see it yet. It'll only be seen when a boat goes out to fish. And we shall be there as early as any boat goes out! I vote we get up at dawn.'

'That's pretty early,' said George. 'Can you wake up? I'm often out at dawn, but you're not used to it.'

'Of course we can wake up,' said Julian. 'Well – here we are back at the beach again – and I'm glad. My arms are really tired and I'm so hungry I could eat a whole cupboard of food.'

'Woof,' said Tim, quite agreeing.

'I'll have to take Tim to Alf,' said George, jumping out of the boat. 'You get the boat in, Julian. I'll join you in a few minutes.'

It wasn't long before all four were sitting down to a good tea. Aunt Fanny had baked new scones for them, and had made a ginger cake with black treacle. It was dark brown and sticky to eat. The children finished it all up and said it was the nicest they had ever tasted.

'Did you have an exciting day?' asked their aunt.

'Oh yes!' said Anne, eagerly. 'The storm was amazing. It threw up . . .'

Julian and Dick both kicked her under the table. George couldn't reach her or she would most certainly have kicked her too. Anne stared at the boys angrily, with tears in her eyes.

'Now what's the matter?' asked Aunt Fanny. 'Did somebody kick you, Anne? Well, really, this kicking under the table has got to stop. Poor Anne will be covered with bruises. What did the sea throw up, Anne?'

'It threw up the most enormous waves,' said Anne, looking defiantly at the others. She knew they had thought she was going to say that the sea had thrown up the wreck – but they were wrong! They had kicked her for nothing!

'Sorry for kicking you, Anne,' said Julian.

'My foot sort of slipped.'

'So did mine,' said Dick. 'Yes, Aunt Fanny, it was incredible. The waves raced up that little inlet on the island, and we had to take our boat almost up to the top of the low cliff there.'

'I wasn't really afraid of the storm,' said Anne. 'In fact, I wasn't really as afraid of it as Ti—'

Everyone knew that Anne was going to mention Timothy, and they all interrupted her at once, speaking very loudly. Julian managed to get a kick in again.

'Oooh!' said Anne.

'The rabbits were so tame,' said Julian, loudly.

'We watched the cormorants,' said Dick, and George joined in too, talking at the same time.

'The jackdaws made such a noise, they said "Chack, chack, chack," all the time.'

'Well, really, you sound like jackdaws yourselves, talking all at once like this!' said Aunt Fanny, with a laugh. 'Now, have you all finished? Very well, then, go and wash your sticky hands – yes, George, I know they're sticky, because I made that ginger cake, and you've had three slices! Then you had better go and play quietly in the other room, because it's raining, and you can't go out. But don't disturb your father, George. He's very busy.'

The children went to wash. 'Idiot!' said Julian to Anne. 'Nearly gave us away twice!'

'I didn't mean what you thought I meant the first time!' began Anne indignantly.

George interrupted her.

'I'd rather you gave the secret of the wreck away than my secret about Tim,' she said. 'You've got a careless tongue.'

'Yes, I have,' said Anne, sorrowfully. 'I think I'd better not talk at meal-times any more. I love Tim so much I just can't seem to help wanting to talk about him.'

They all went to play in the other room. Julian turned a table upside down with a crash. 'We'll play at wrecks,' he said. 'This is the wreck. Now we're going to explore it.'

The door flew open and an angry, frowning face looked in. It was George's father!

'What was that noise?' he said. 'George! Did you overturn that table?'

'I did,' said Julian. 'I'm sorry. I forgot you were working.'

'Any more noise like that and I'll keep you all

in tomorrow!' said his Uncle Quentin. 'Georgina, keep your cousins quiet.'

The door shut and Uncle Quentin went out. The children looked at one another.

'Your dad's pretty fierce, isn't he?' said Julian. 'I'm sorry I made that noise. I didn't think.'

'We'd better do something really quiet,' said George. 'Or he'll keep his word – and we'll find ourselves inside tomorrow just when we want to explore the wreck.'

This was a terrible thought. Anne went to get some cards to play Patience with. Julian fetched a book. George picked up a beautiful little boat she was carving out of a piece of wood. Dick lay back on a chair and thought of the exciting wreck. The rain poured down steadily, and everyone hoped it would have stopped by the morning.

'We'll have to be up incredibly early,' said Dick, yawning. 'How about going to bed in good time tonight? I'm tired after all that rowing.'

Normally none of the children liked going to bed early – but with such an exciting thing to look forward to, early bed seemed different that night.

'It'll make the time go quickly,' said Anne,

putting down her cards. 'Shall we go now?'

'What do you think Mum would say if we went just after tea?' said George. 'She'd think we were all ill. No, let's go after supper. We'll just say we're tired with rowing – which is true – and we'll get a good night's sleep, and be ready for our adventure tomorrow morning. And it is an adventure, you know. It isn't many people that have the chance of exploring an old, old wreck like that, which has always been at the bottom of the sea!'

So, by eight o'clock, all the children were in bed, much to Aunt Fanny's surprise. Anne fell asleep at once. Julian and Dick were not long – but George lay awake for some time, thinking of her island, her wreck – and, of course, her beloved dog!

'I must take Tim too,' she thought, as she fell asleep. 'We can't leave old Tim out of this. He shall share in the adventure too!'

8 *Exploring the wreck*

Julian woke first the next morning. He awoke just as the sun was slipping over the horizon in the east, and filling the sky with gold. Julian stared at the ceiling for a moment, and then, in a rush, he remembered all that had happened the day before. He sat up straight in bed and whispered as loudly as he could.

'Dick! Wake up! We're going to see the wreck! Wake up!'

Dick woke and grinned at Julian. A feeling of happiness crept over him. They were going on an adventure. He leapt out of bed and ran quietly to the girls' room. He opened the door. Both the girls were fast asleep, Anne curled up like a dormouse under the sheet.

Dick shook George and then dug Anne in the back. They awoke and sat up. 'Come on!' whispered Dick. 'The sun is just rising. We'll have to hurry.'

George's blue eyes shone as she dressed. Anne skipped about quietly, finding her few clothes – just a swimming costume, jeans and jumper – and trainers for her feet. It wasn't many minutes before they were all ready.

'Now, not a creak on the stairs – not a cough or a giggle!' warned Julian, as they stood together on the landing. Anne was a dreadful giggler, and had often given secret plans away by her sudden explosive choke. But this time she was as solemn as the others, and as careful. They crept down the stairs and undid the little front door. Not a sound was made. They shut the door quietly and made their way down the garden path to the gate. The gate always creaked, so they climbed over it instead of opening it.

The sun was now shining brightly, though it was still low in the eastern sky. It felt warm already. The sky was so beautifully blue that Anne couldn't help feeling it had been freshly washed! 'It looks just as if it's come out of the washing machine,' she told the others.

They squealed with laughter at her. She did say odd things at times. But they knew what she meant. The day had a lovely new feeling about it

– the clouds were pink in the bright blue sky, and the sea looked smooth and fresh. It was impossible to imagine that it had been so rough the day before.

George got her boat. Then she went to get Tim, while the boys hauled the boat down to the sea. Alf was surprised to see George so early. He was about to go with his father, fishing. He grinned at George.

'You going fishing, too?' he said to her. 'Hey, wasn't that a storm yesterday! I thought you'd be caught in it.'

'We were,' said George. 'Come on, Tim! Come on!'

Tim was very pleased to see George so early. He capered round her as she ran back to the others, almost tripping her up as she went. He leapt into the boat as soon as he saw it, and stood at the stern, his red tongue out, his tail wagging violently.

'It's a wonder his tail stays on,' said Anne, looking at it. 'One day, Timothy, you'll wag it right off.'

They set off to the island. It was easy to row now, because the sea was so calm. They came to the island, and rowed around it to the other side.

And there was the wreck, piled high on some sharp rocks! It had settled down now and did not stir as waves slid under it. It lay a little to one side, and the broken mast, now shorter than before, stuck out at an angle.

'There she is,' said Julian, in excitement. 'Poor old wreck! I guess she's a bit more battered now. What a noise she made when she went crashing on to those rocks yesterday!'

'How do we get to her?' asked Anne, looking at the mass of ugly, sharp rocks all around. But George wasn't worried. She knew almost every inch of the coast around her little island. She pulled steadily at the oars and soon came near to the rocks in which the great wreck rested.

The children looked at the wreck from their boat. It was big, much bigger than they had imagined when they had peered at it from the top of the water. It was encrusted with shellfish of some kind, and strands of brown and green seaweed hung down. It smelt funny. It had great holes in its sides, showing where it had battered against rocks. There were holes in the deck too. Altogether, it looked a sad and forlorn old ship –

but to the four children it was the most exciting thing in the whole world.

They rowed to the rocks on which the wreck lay. The tide washed over them. George took a look round.

'We'll tie our boat up to the wreck itself,' she said. 'And we'll easily get on to the deck by climbing up the side. Look, Julian! – throw this loop of rope over that broken bit of wood there, sticking out from the side.'

Julian did as he was told. The rope tightened and the boat was held in position. Then George clambered up the side of the wreck like a monkey. She was wonderful at climbing. Julian and Dick followed her, but Anne had to be helped up. Soon all four were standing on the slanting deck. It was slippery with seaweed, and the smell was very strong indeed. Anne didn't like it.

'Well, this was the deck,' said George, 'and that's where the men got up and down.' She pointed to a large hole. They went to it and looked down. The remains of an iron ladder were still there. George looked at it.

'I think it's still strong enough to hold us,' she said. 'I'll go first. Anyone got a torch? It looks pretty dark down there.'

Julian had a torch. He handed it to George. The children became rather quiet. It was mysterious somehow to look down into the dark inside of the big ship. What would they find? George switched on the torch and then swung herself down the ladder. The others followed.

The light from the torch showed a very strange sight. The under-parts of the ship were low-ceilinged, made of thick oak. The children had to bend their heads to get about. It seemed as if there were places that might have been cabins, though it was difficult to tell now, for everything was so battered, sea-drenched and seaweedy. The smell was really horrible, though it was mostly of drying seaweed.

The children slipped about on the seaweed as they went round the inside of the ship. It didn't seem so big inside after all. There was a big hold under the cabins, which the children saw by the light of their torch.

'That's where the boxes of gold would have been kept, I expect,' said Julian. But there was nothing in the hold except water and fish! The children couldn't go down because the water was too deep. One or two barrels floated in the water, but they had burst open and were empty.

'I expect they were water-barrels, or barrels of pork or biscuit,' said George. 'Let's go round the other part of the ship again – where the cabins are. Isn't it strange to see bunks there that sailors have slept in? – and look at that old wooden chair. Just think of it still being here after all these years! Look at the things on those hooks too – they are all rusty now, and covered with seaweedy stuff – but they must have been the cook's pans and dishes!'

It was a very weird trip round the old wreck. The children were all on the look-out for boxes which might contain bars of gold – but there didn't seem to be one single box of any kind anywhere!

They came to a bigger cabin than the others. It had a bunk in one corner, in which a large crab rested. An old bit of furniture looking rather like a table with two legs, all encrusted with greyish shells, lay against the bunk. Wooden shelves, festooned with grey-green seaweed, hung crookedly on the walls of the cabin.

'This must have been the captain's own cabin,'

said Julian. 'It's the biggest one. Look, what's that in the corner?'

'An old cup!' said Anne, picking it up. 'And here's half of a saucer. I expect the captain was sitting here having a cup of tea when the ship went down.'

This made the children feel rather uneasy. It was dark and smelly in the little cabin, and the floor was wet and slippery to their feet. George began to feel that her wreck was really more pleasant sunk under the water than raised above it!

'Let's go,' she said, with a shiver. 'I don't like it much. It is exciting, I know – but it's a bit creepy too.'

They turned to go. Julian flashed his torch round the little cabin for the last time. He was about to switch it off and follow the others up to the deck above when he caught sight of something that made him stop. He flashed his torch on to it, and then called to the others.

'Hang on! There's a cupboard here in the wall. Let's see if there's anything in it!'

The others turned back and looked. They saw what looked like a small cupboard set in level with the wall of the cabin. What had caught Julian's eye was the keyhole. There was no key there, though.

'There just *might* be something inside,' said Julian. He tried to prise open the wooden door with his fingers, but it wouldn't move. 'It's locked,' he said. 'Of course it would be!'

'I expect the lock is rotten by now,' said George, and she tried too. Then she took out her penknife and inserted it between the cupboard door and the cabin-wall. She forced back the blade – and the lock of the cupboard suddenly snapped! As she had said, it was completely rotten. The door swung open, and the children saw a shelf inside with a few curious things on it.

There was a wooden box, swollen with the wet sea-water in which it had lain for years. There were two or three things that looked like old, pulpy books. There was a glass, cracked in half – and two or three strange objects so spoilt by sea-water that no one could possibly say what they were.

'Nothing very interesting – except the box,' said Julian, and he picked it up. 'Anyway, I expect that whatever is inside is ruined. But we may as well try and open it.'

He and George tried their best to force the lock of the old wooden box. On the top of it were stamped initials – H.J.K.

'I expect those were the captain's initials,' said Dick.

'No, they were the initials of my great-great-great-grandfather!' said George, her eyes shining suddenly. 'I've heard all about him. His name was Henry John Kirrin. This was his ship, you know. This must have been his private box, where he kept his old papers or diaries. Oh – we have to open it!'

But it was impossible to force the lid up with the tools they had there. They soon gave it up, and Julian picked up the box to carry it to the boat.

'We'll open it at home,' he said, sounding excited. 'We'll get a hammer or something, and get it open somehow. What a find!'

They all felt that they really had something mysterious in their possession. Was there anything inside the box – and if so, what would it be? They longed to get home and open it!

They went up on deck, climbing the old iron

ladder. As soon as they got there they saw that others besides themselves had discovered that the wreck had been thrown up from the bottom of the sea!

'Half the fishing-boats of the bay have found it!' cried Julian, looking round at the fishing-boats that had come as near as they dared to the wreck. The fishermen were looking at the wreck in amazement. When they saw the children on board they called to them loudly.

'Ahoy there! What's that ship?'

'It's the old wreck!' yelled back Julian. 'She was thrown up yesterday in the storm!'

'Don't say any more,' said George, frowning. 'It's *my* wreck. I don't want sightseers on it!'

So no more was said, and the four children got into their boat and rowed home as fast as they could. It was past their breakfast-time. They might get told off. They might even be sent to bed by George's fierce father – but what did they care? They had explored the wreck – and had come away with a box which *might* contain – well, if not bars of gold, one *small* bar, perhaps!

They did get told off. They had to go without half their breakfast, too, because Uncle Quentin said that children who came in so late didn't deserve hot bacon and eggs – only toast and marmalade.

They hid the box under the bed in the boys' room. Tim had been left with Alf – or rather, had been tied up in his back garden, for Alf had gone out fishing, and was even now gazing from his father's boat at the strange wreck.

'We can make a bit of money taking sightseers out to this wreck,' said Alf. And before the day was out dozens of interested people had seen the old wreck from the decks of motor-boats and fishing-boats.

George was furious about it. But she couldn't do anything. After all, as Julian said, anybody could have a look!

9 *The box from the wreck*

The first thing that the children did after breakfast was to fetch the precious box and take it out to the tool-shed in the garden. They were longing to force it open. All of them secretly felt certain that it would hold treasure of some sort.

Julian looked round for a tool. He found a chisel and decided that would be just the thing to force the box open. He tried, but the tool slipped and jabbed his fingers. Then he tried other things, but the box obstinately refused to open. The children stared at it crossly.

'I know what to do,' said Anne at last. 'Let's take it to the top of the house and throw it down to the ground. I expect it would burst open.'

The others thought over the idea. 'It might be worth trying,' said Julian. 'The only thing is it might break or spoil anything inside the box.'

But there didn't seem any other way to open the box, so Julian carried it up to the top of the house. He went to the attic and opened the window there. The others were down below, waiting. Julian hurled the box out of the window as violently as he could. It flew through the air and landed with a crash on the patio below.

At once the french window there opened and their Uncle Quentin came out like a bullet from a gun.

'What are you doing?' he cried. 'Surely you aren't throwing things at each other out of the window? What's this on the ground?'

The children looked at the box. It had burst open and lay on the ground, showing a waterproof tin lining. Whatever was in the box would not be spoilt! It would be quite dry!

Dick ran to pick it up.

'I said, what's this on the ground?' shouted his uncle and moved towards him.

'It's – it's something that belongs to us,' said Dick, going red.

'Well, I'll take it away from you,' said his uncle. 'Disturbing me like this! Give it to me. Where did you get it?'

Nobody answered. Uncle Quentin frowned till his glasses nearly fell off. 'Where did you get it?' he barked, glaring at poor Anne, who was nearest.

'Out of the wreck,' stammered the little girl, scared.

'Out of the wreck!' said her uncle, in surprise. 'The old wreck that was thrown up yesterday? I heard about that. Do you mean to say you've been in it?'

'Yes,' said Dick. Julian joined them at that moment, looking worried. It would be awful if his uncle took the box just as they got it open. But that was exactly what he did!

'Well, this box may contain something important,' he said, and he took it from Dick's hands. 'You've no right to go prying about in that old wreck. You might take something that mattered.'

'Well, it's my wreck,' said George, in a defiant tone. 'Please, Dad, let us have the box. We'd just got it opened. We thought it might hold – a gold bar – or something like that!'

'A gold bar!' said her father, with a snort. 'What a baby you are! This small box would never hold a thing like that! It's much more likely to contain particulars of what happened to the bars! I have always thought that the gold was safely delivered somewhere – and that the ship, empty of its valuable cargo, got wrecked as it left the bay!'

'Oh, Dad – please, please let us have our box,' begged George, almost in tears. She suddenly felt certain that it did contain papers that might tell them what had happened to the gold. But without another word her father turned and went into the house, carrying the box, burst open and cracked, its tin lining showing through under his arm.

Anne burst into tears. 'Don't blame me for telling him we got it from the wreck,' she sobbed. 'Please don't. He looked so angry. I just had to tell him.'

'It's all right,' said Julian, putting his arm round Anne. He looked furious. He thought it was very unfair of his uncle to take the box like that. 'Listen – I'm not going to put up with this. We'll get hold of that box somehow and look into it. I'm sure your dad won't bother himself with it, George – he'll start writing his book again and forget all about it. I'll wait my chance and slip into his study and get it, even if it means a telling off if I'm discovered!'

'Good!' said George. 'We'll all keep a watch and see if Dad goes out.'

So they took it in turns to keep watch, but most annoyingly their Uncle Quentin remained in his study all the morning. Aunt Fanny was surprised to see one or two children always about the garden that day, instead of down on the beach.

'Why don't you all keep together and go swimming or something?' she said. 'Have you quarrelled with one another?'

'No,' said Dick. 'Of course not.' But he didn't say why they were in the garden!

'Doesn't your dad *ever* go out?' he said to George, when it was her turn to keep watch. 'I don't think he leads a very healthy life.'

'Scientists never do,' said George, as if she knew all about them. 'But I tell you what – he may go to sleep this afternoon! He sometimes does!'

Julian was left behind in the garden that afternoon. He sat down under a tree and opened a book. Soon he heard a noise that made him look up. He knew at once what it was!

'That's Uncle Quentin snoring!' he said in excitement. 'I wonder if I could creep in at the french window and get our box!'

He went over to the windows and looked in. One was a little way open and Julian opened it a little more. He saw his uncle lying back in a comfortable armchair, his mouth a little open, his eyes closed, fast asleep! Every time he took a breath, he snored.

'He's fast asleep,' thought the boy. 'And there's the box, just behind him, on that table. I'll risk it. I'll get into huge trouble if I'm caught, but I can't help that!'

He crept in. His uncle still snored. He tiptoed by him to the table behind his uncle's chair. He took hold of the box.

And then a bit of the broken wood of the box fell to the floor with a thud! His uncle stirred in his chair and opened his eyes. Quick as lightning the boy crouched down behind his uncle's chair, hardly breathing.

'What's that?' he heard his uncle say. Julian didn't move. Then his uncle settled down again and shut his eyes. Soon there was the sound of his rhythmic snoring!

'That's lucky!' thought Julian. 'He's off again!'

Quietly he stood up, holding the box. On tiptoe he crept to the french window. He slipped out and ran softly down the garden path. He didn't think of hiding the box. All he wanted to do was to get to the other children and show them what he had done!

He ran to the beach where the others were lying in the sun. 'Hey!' he yelled. 'Hey! I've got it! I've got it!'

They all sat up with a jerk, thrilled to see the box in Julian's arms. They forgot all about the other people on the beach. Julian dropped down on the sand and grinned.

'Your dad went to sleep,' he said to George. 'Tim, don't lick me like that! And I went in – and a bit of the box dropped on the floor – and it woke him up!'

'Oh no!' said George. 'What happened?'

'I crouched down behind his chair till he went to sleep again,' said Julian. 'Then I ran for it. Now – let's see what's in here. I don't believe your dad's even looked!'

He hadn't. The tin lining was intact. It had rusted with the years of lying in the wet, and the lid was so tightly fitted down that it was almost impossible to move it.

But once George began to work at it with her

penknife, scraping away the rust, it began to loosen – and in about a quarter of an hour it came off!

The children bent eagerly over it. Inside lay some old papers and a book of some kind with a black cover. Nothing else at all. No bar of gold. No treasure. Everyone felt a bit disappointed.

'It's not even damp,' said Julian, surprised. 'The tin lining kept everything completely dry.'

He picked up the book and opened it. 'It's a diary your great-great-great-grandfather kept of the ship's voyages,' he said. 'I can hardly read the writing. It's so small and old-fashioned.'

George picked up one of the papers. It was made of thick parchment, quite yellow with age. She spread it out on the sand and looked at it. The others glanced at it too, but they couldn't tell what it was. It seemed to be a kind of map.

'Perhaps it's a map of some place he had to go to,' said Julian. But suddenly George's hands began to shake as she held the map, and her eyes shone as she looked up at the others. She opened her mouth but didn't speak.

'What's the matter?' asked Julian. 'Lost your voice?'

George shook her head and then began to speak with a rush. 'Julian, this is a map of my old castle – of Kirrin Castle – when it wasn't a ruin! It shows the dungeons – and look what's written here!'

She put a trembling finger on one part of the dungeons map and the others leaned over to see what it was. There, in old-fashioned writing, was a single, strange word.

INGOTS

'Ingots!' said Anne, puzzled. 'What does that mean? I've never heard that word before.'

But the two boys had. 'Ingots!' Dick exclaimed. 'That must mean the bars of gold! They were called ingots.'

'Most bars of metal are called ingots,' said Julian, going red with excitement. 'But we know that there's gold missing from that ship, so it really looks as if ingots here means bars of gold. Just think – they might still be hidden underneath Kirrin Castle. George, isn't it amazing!'

George nodded, shaking with excitement. 'If only we could find it!' she whispered. 'Just imagine!'

'We'll have a proper hunt for it,' said Julian. 'It'll be really difficult because of the castle being in ruins, and so overgrown. But somehow we'll find those ingots. What a brilliant word. Ingots! Ingots! Ingots!'

It sounded much more exciting than the word gold. Nobody spoke about gold any more. They talked about the ingots. Tim couldn't make out what the excitement was at all. He wagged his tail and tried hard to lick first one and then another of the children, but for once not one of them paid any attention to him! He simply couldn't understand it, and after a while he went and sat down by himself with his back to the children, and his ears down.

'Oh, look at poor Timothy!' said George. 'He can't understand why we're so excited. Tim! Tim, it's all right, you're not in trouble or anything. Oh, Tim, we've got the most wonderful secret in the whole world.'

Tim bounded up, his tail wagging, pleased to be taken notice of once more. He put his big paw on the precious map, and the four children shouted at him at once.

'We can't have that torn!' said Julian. Then he

looked at the others and frowned. 'What are we going to do about the box?' he said. 'I mean – George's dad is bound to miss it, isn't he? We'll have to give it back.'

'Can't we take out the map and keep it?' said Dick. 'He won't know it was there if he hasn't looked in the box, and we're pretty sure he hasn't. The other things don't matter much – they're only that old diary and a few letters.'

'To be on the safe side, let's take a copy of the map,' said Julian. 'Then we can put the real map back and replace the box.'

They all voted that a very good idea. They went back to Kirrin Cottage and traced out the map carefully. They did it in the tool-shed because they didn't want anyone to see them. It was a strange map. It was in three parts.

'This part shows the dungeons under the castle,' said Julian. 'And this shows a plan of the ground floor of the castle – and this shows the top part. It must have been an amazing place in those days! The dungeons run all under the castle. I bet they were pretty awful places. I wonder how people got down to them.'

'We'll have to study the map a bit more and

see,' said George. 'It all looks rather muddled at the moment – but once we take the map over to the castle and study it there, we might be able to work out how to get down to the hidden dungeons. Ooooh! I bet no other kids ever had an adventure like this.'

Julian put the traced map carefully into his jeans pocket. He didn't intend to let go of it. It was very precious. Then he put the real map back into the box and looked towards the house. 'What about putting it back now?' he said. 'Maybe your dad is still asleep, George.'

But he wasn't. He was awake. Luckily he hadn't missed the box! He came into the dining-room to have tea with the family, and Julian took his chance. He muttered an excuse, slipped away from the table, and replaced the box on the table behind his uncle's chair!

He winked at the others when he came back. They felt relieved. They were all scared of Uncle Quentin, and were not at all keen to be in his bad books. Anne didn't say one word during the whole of the meal. She was worried she might give something away, either about Tim or the box. The others spoke very little too. While they were eating the phone rang and Aunt Fanny went to answer it.

She soon came back. 'It's for you, Quentin,' she said. 'That old wreck has caused quite a lot of excitement. There are some journalists wanting to ask you questions about it.'

'Tell them I'll see them at six,' said Uncle Quentin. The children looked at one another in alarm. They hoped that their uncle wouldn't show the box to the journalists. Then the secret of the hidden gold might come out!

'It's lucky we took a tracing of the map!' said Julian, after tea. 'But I'm sorry now we left the real map in the box. Someone else may guess our secret!'

10 An astonishing offer

The next morning the papers were full of the extraordinary way in which the old wreck had been thrown up out of the sea. The journalists had got out of the children's uncle the tale of the wreck and the lost gold, and some of them even managed to land on Kirrin Island and take pictures of the old ruined castle.

George was furious. 'It's my castle!' she stormed to her mother. 'It's my island. You said it could be mine. You did, you did!'

'I know, George,' said her mother. 'But you really must be sensible. It can't hurt the island to be landed on, and it can't hurt the castle to be photographed.'

'But I don't want it to be,' said George, her face dark and sulky. 'It's mine. And the wreck is mine. You said so.'

'Well, I didn't know it was going to be thrown up like that,' said her mother. 'Do be sensible,

George. What can it possibly matter if people go to look at the wreck? You can't stop them.'

George couldn't stop them, but that didn't make her any the less angry about it. The children were astonished at the interest that the cast-up wreck caused, and because of that, Kirrin Island became an object of great interest too. Sightseers came to see it from all around, and the fishermen managed to find the little inlet and land the people there. George sobbed with rage, and Julian tried to comfort her.

'Listen, George! No one knows our secret yet. We'll wait till this excitement has died down, and then we'll go to Kirrin Castle and find the ingots.'

'If someone doesn't find them first,' said George, drying her eyes. She was furious with herself for crying, but she really couldn't help it.

'How could they?' said Julian. 'No one has seen inside the box yet! I'm going to wait my chance and get that map out before anyone sees it!'

But he didn't have a chance, because something terrible happened. Uncle Quentin sold the old box to a man who bought antiques! He came out from his study, beaming, a day or two after the excitement began, and told Aunt Fanny and the children.

'I've struck a very good bargain with that man,' he said to his wife. 'You know that old tin-lined box from the wreck? Well, this fellow collects curious things like that, and he gave me a very good price for it. Very good indeed. More even than I could expect for the writing of my book! As soon as he saw the old map there and the old diary he said at once that he would buy the whole collection.'

The children stared at him in horror. The box was sold! Now someone would study that map and perhaps guess what 'ingots' meant. The story of the lost gold had been put into all the newspapers now. Nobody could fail to know what the map showed if they studied it carefully.

The children did not dare to tell Uncle Quentin what they knew. It was true he was all smiles now, and was promising to buy them new shrimping-nets, and even a raft – but he was such an unpredictable person. He might fly into a furious temper if he heard that Julian had taken the box and opened it himself, while his uncle was sleeping.

When they were alone the children discussed the whole matter. It seemed very serious indeed. They half-wondered if they should let Aunt Fanny into the secret – but it was such a precious secret, and so exciting, that they felt they didn't want to give it away to anyone at all.

'Listen!' said Julian, at last. 'We'll ask Aunt Fanny if we can go to Kirrin Island and spend a day or two there – sleep there at night too, I mean. That will give us a little time to poke round and see what we can find. The sightseers will stop coming after a day or two, I'm sure. Maybe we'll get in before anyone finds out our secret. After all, the man who bought the box may not even guess that the map shows Kirrin Castle.'

They felt more cheerful. It was so awful to do nothing. As soon as they had planned to act, they felt better. They decided to ask their aunt the next day if they might go and spend the weekend at the castle. The weather was glorious, and it would be great fun. They could take plenty of food with them.

When they went to ask Aunt Fanny, Uncle Quentin was with her. He was all smiles again, and even clapped Julian on the back. 'Well!' he said. 'What's this deputation for?'

'We just wanted to ask Aunt Fanny something,' said Julian, politely. 'Aunt Fanny, as the weather is so good, will you let us go for the weekend to Kirrin Castle, please, and spend a day or two there on the island? We'd really love to!'

'Well – what do you think, Quentin?' asked their aunt, turning to her husband.

'If they want to, they can,' said Uncle Quentin. 'They won't have a chance to, soon. We've had an amazing offer for Kirrin Island! A man wants to buy it, rebuild the castle as a hotel, and make it into a proper holiday place! What do you think of that?'

All four children stared at the smiling man, shocked and horrified. Somebody was going to buy the island! Had their secret been discovered? Did the man want to buy the castle because he had read the map, and knew there was plenty of gold hidden there?

George made a strange choking sound. Her eyes burned as if they were on fire. 'Mum! You can't sell my island! You can't sell my castle! I won't let them be sold.'

Her father frowned. 'Don't be silly, Georgina,'

he said. 'It isn't really yours. You know that. It belongs to your mother, and naturally she'd like to sell it if she could. We need the money very badly. You'll be able to have lots of nice things once we sell the island.'

'I don't want nice things!' cried poor George. 'My castle and my island are the nicest things I could ever have. Mum! You *said* I could have them. You know you did! I believed you.'

'George, I did mean you to have them to play on, when I thought they couldn't possibly be worth anything,' said her mother, looking very upset. 'But now things are different. We've been offered quite a good sum, far more than we ever thought of getting – and we really can't afford to turn it down.'

'So you only gave me the island when you thought it wasn't worth anything,' said George, her face white and angry. 'As soon as it's worth money you take it away again. I think that's horrible. It – it isn't *honest*.'

'That's enough, Georgina,' said her father, angrily. 'You're only a child. Your mother didn't really mean what she said – it was only to please you. But you know well enough you'll share in the money we get and have anything you want.'

'I won't touch a penny!' said George, in a low choking voice. 'You'll be sorry you sold it.'

The girl turned and stumbled out of the room. The others felt very sorry for her. They knew what she was feeling. She took things so very seriously. Julian thought she didn't understand grown-ups very well. It wasn't any use fighting grown-ups. They could do exactly as they liked. If they wanted to take away George's island and castle, they could. If they wanted to sell it, they could! But what Uncle Quentin didn't know was the fact that there might be a store of gold ingots there! Julian stared at his uncle and wondered whether to warn him. Then he decided not to. There was just a chance that the four children could find the gold first!

'When are you selling the island, Uncle?' he asked quietly.

'The deeds will be signed in about a week's time,' was the answer. 'So if you really want to spend a day or two there, you'd better do so quickly, for after that you may not get permission from the new owners.'

'Was it the man who bought the old box who

wants to buy the island?' asked Julian.

'Yes,' said his uncle. 'I was a little surprised myself, because I thought he was just a buyer of antiques. I was astonished that he had the idea of buying the island to rebuild the castle as a hotel. Still, I suppose there will be big money in running a hotel there – very romantic, staying on a little island like that – people will like it. I'm no businessman myself, and I certainly wouldn't want to invest my money in a place like Kirrin Island. But I should think he knows what he's doing all right.'

'I'll bet he does,' thought Julian to himself, as he went out of the room with Dick and Anne. 'He's read that map – and has jumped to the same idea that we did – the store of hidden ingots is somewhere on that island – and he's going to get it! He doesn't want to build a hotel! He's after the treasure! I expect he's offered Uncle Quentin some silly low price that poor old Uncle thinks is wonderful! What a horrible thing to happen.'

He went to find George. She was in the tool-shed, looking quite green. She said she felt sick.

'It's only because you're so upset,' said Julian. He put his arm round her. For once George didn't push it away. She felt comforted. Tears came into her eyes, and she angrily tried to blink them away.

'Listen, George!' said Julian. 'We mustn't give up hope. We'll go to Kirrin Island tomorrow, and we'll do our very, very best to get down into the dungeons somehow and find the ingots. We'll stay there till we do. OK? Now cheer up, because we'll want your help in planning everything. Thank goodness we took a tracing of the map.'

George cheered up a little. She still felt angry with her parents, but the thought of going to Kirrin Island for a day or two, and taking Timothy too, certainly seemed good.

'I do think my mum and dad are unkind,' she said.

'Well, they're not really,' said Julian, trying to be fair. 'After all, if they need money badly, they'd be silly not to sell something they think is useless. And you know, your dad did say you could have anything you want. I know what I'd ask for, if I were you!'

'What?' asked George.

'Timothy, of course!' said Julian. And that made George smile and cheer up!

11 *Off to Kirrin Island*

Julian and George went to find Dick and Anne. They were waiting for them in the garden, looking upset. They were glad to see Julian and George and ran to meet them.

Anne took George's hands. 'I'm so sorry about your island, George,' she said.

'So am I,' said Dick.

George managed to smile. 'I've been acting like a girl,' she said, half-ashamed. 'But I did get an awful shock.'

Julian told the others what they had planned. 'We'll go tomorrow morning,' he said. 'We'll make out a list of all the things we shall need. Let's start right now.'

He took out a pencil and notebook. The others looked at him.

'Things to eat,' said Dick at once. 'Plenty because we'll be hungry.'

'Something to drink,' said George. 'There's no

water on the island – though I think there was a well or something, years ago, that went right down below the level of the sea, and was fresh water. Anyway, I've never found it.'

'Food,' wrote down Julian, 'and drink.' He looked at the others.

'Spades,' he said solemnly, and scribbled the word down.

Anne stared in surprise.

'What for?' she asked.

'Well, we'll want to dig about when we're hunting for a way down to the dungeons,' said Julian.

'Ropes,' said Dick. 'We may want those too.'

'And torches,' said George. 'It'll be dark in the dungeons.'

'Oooh!' said Anne, feeling a pleasant shiver go down her back at the thought. She had no idea what dungeons were like, but they sounded exciting.

'Rugs,' said Dick. 'We'll be cold at night if we sleep in that little old room.'

Julian wrote them down. 'Mugs to drink from,' he said. 'And we'll take a few tools too – we may perhaps need them. You never know.'

At the end of half an hour they had a long list, and everyone felt pleased and excited. George was beginning to recover from her rage and disappointment. If she had been alone, and had brooded over everything, she would have been in an even worse sulk and temper – but somehow the others were so calm and sensible and cheerful. It was impossible to sulk for long if she was with them.

'I think I'd have been much nicer if I hadn't been on my own so much,' thought George to herself, as she looked at Julian's bent head. 'Talking about things to other people does help a lot. They don't seem so dreadful then; they seem more bearable and ordinary. I really like my three cousins. I like them because they talk and laugh and are always cheerful and kind. I wish I were like them. I'm sulky and bad-tempered and fierce, and no wonder Dad gets cross with me and tells me off so often. Mum's lovely, but I understand now why she says I'm difficult. I'm different from my cousins – they're easy to understand, and everyone likes them. I'm glad they came. They are making me more like I ought to be.'

This was a long thought to think, and George

looked very serious while she was thinking it. Julian looked up and caught her blue eyes fixed on him. He smiled.

'Penny for your thoughts!' he said.

'They're not worth a penny,' said George, going red. 'I was just thinking how nice you all are – and how I wished I could be like you.'

'You're nice too,' said Julian, surprisingly. 'You've just been on your own a bit too much, that's all. I think you're a really interesting person.'

George flushed red again, and felt pleased. 'Let's go and take Timothy for a walk,' she said. 'He'll be wondering what's happened to us today.'

They all went off together, and Timothy greeted them at the top of his voice. They told him all about their plans for the next day, and he wagged his tail and looked up at them out of his soft brown eyes as if he understood every single word they said!

'He must feel pleased to think he's going to be with us for two or three days,' said Anne.

It was very exciting the next morning, setting off in the boat with all their things packed neatly at one end. Julian checked them all by reading out aloud from his list. It didn't seem as if they had forgotten anything.

'Got the map?' said Dick, suddenly.

Julian nodded.

'I put on clean jeans this morning,' he said, 'but I remembered to put the map into my pocket. Here it is!'

He took it out – and the wind blew it right out of his hands! It fell into the sea and bobbed there in the wind. All four children gave a cry of utter dismay. Their precious map!

'Quick! Row after it!' cried George, and swung the boat round. But someone was quicker than she was! Tim had seen the paper fly from Julian's hand, and had heard and understood the cries of dismay. With an enormous splash he leapt into the water and swam valiantly after the map.

He could swim well for a dog, for he was strong and powerful. He soon had the map in his mouth and was swimming back to the boat. The children thought he was a hero!

George hauled him into the boat and took the map from his mouth. There was hardly the mark of his teeth on it, he had carried it so carefully! It was wet, and the children looked anxiously at it to see if the tracing had been spoilt. But Julian had traced it very strongly, and it was quite all right. He placed it on a seat to dry, and told Dick to hold it there in the sun.

'That was close!' he said, and the others agreed.

George took the oars again, and they set off once more for the island, getting a shower from Timothy when he stood up and shook his wet coat. He was given a big biscuit as a reward, and crunched it up with great enjoyment.

George made her way through the reefs of rocks with a sure hand. The others thought it was amazing how she could slide the boat in between the dangerous rocks and never get a scratch. They thought she was really wonderful. She brought them safely to the little inlet, and they jumped out on to the sand. They pulled the boat high up, in case the tide came far up the tiny cove, and then began to unload their goods.

'We'll carry all the things to that little stone room,' said Julian. 'They'll be safe there and won't get wet if it rains. I hope nobody comes to the island while we are here, George.'

'I shouldn't think they would,' said George. 'Dad said it would be about a week before the deeds were signed, making over the island to that man. It won't be his till then. We've got a week, anyhow.'

'Well, we don't need to keep a watch then,' said Julian, who had half thought that it would be a good idea to make someone stay on guard at the inlet, to give a warning to the others in case anyone else arrived. 'Come on! You take the spades, Dick. I'll take the food and drink with George. And Anne can take the little things.'

The food and drink were in a big box, for the children did not mean to starve while they were on the island! They had brought loaves of bread, butter, biscuits, jam, tins of fruit, ripe plums, bottles of ginger-beer, a kettle to make tea, and anything else they could think of! George and Julian staggered up the cliff with the heavy box. They had to put it down once or twice to give themselves a rest!

They put everything into the little room. Then they went back to get the collection of blankets and rugs from the boat. They arranged them in the corners of the little room, and thought that it would be very exciting to spend the night there.

'The two girls can sleep together on this pile of

rugs,' said Julian. 'And we two boys will have this pile.'

George looked as if she didn't want to be put with Anne, and classed as a girl. But Anne didn't wish to sleep alone in her corner, and she looked so pleadingly at George that the older girl smiled at her and made no objection. Anne thought that George was getting nicer and nicer!

'Let's get down to business,' said Julian, and he pulled out his map. 'We must study this really carefully, and work out exactly where the entrances to the dungeons are. Now – come around and let's do our best to find out! It's up to us to use our brains – and beat that man who's bought the island!'

They all bent over the traced map. It was quite dry now, and the children looked at it earnestly. It was plain that in the old days the castle had been a very grand place.

'Look,' said Julian, putting his finger on the plan of the dungeons. 'These seem to run all along under the castle – and here – and – here – are some marks that seem to show steps or stairs.'

'Yes,' said George. 'I think they are. It looks as if there are two ways of getting down into the dungeons. One lot of steps seems to begin somewhere near this little room – and the other seems to start under the tower there. What do you think this thing is here, Julian?'

She put her finger on a round hole that was shown not only in the plan of the dungeons, but also in the plan of the ground floor of the castle.

'I can't imagine what that is,' said Julian, puzzled. 'Oh yes, I know what it might be! You said there was an old well somewhere, do you remember? Maybe that's it. It'd have to be very deep to get fresh water from under the sea – so it probably goes down through the dungeons too. Isn't it exciting?'

Everyone thought it was. They felt thrilled and happy. There was definitely something to discover – something they had to discover within the next day or two.

They looked at one another. 'Well,' said Dick,' what are we going to start on? Shall we try to find the entrance to the dungeons – the one that seems to start round about this little room? For all we know there may be a big stone we can lift that opens above the dungeon steps!'

This was a thrilling thought, and the children

jumped up at once. Julian folded up the precious map and put it into his pocket. He looked round. The stone floor of the little room was overgrown with creeping weeds. They had to be cleared away before it was possible to see if there were any stones that looked as if they could be moved.

'We'd better get to work,' said Julian, and he picked up a spade. 'Let's clear away these weeds with our spades – scrape them off, look, like this – and then examine every single stone!'

They all picked up spades and soon the little stone room was full of a scraping sound as the four of them chiselled away at the close-growing weeds with their spades. It wasn't very difficult to get the stones clear of them, and the children worked quickly and eagerly.

Tim got most excited about everything. He hadn't any idea at all what they were doing, but he joined in valiantly. He scraped away at the floor with his four paws, sending earth and plants flying high into the air!

'Tim!' said Julian, shaking a clod of earth out of his hair. 'You're being a bit too enthusiastic. You'll send the stones flying into the air too, in a minute. Isn't it great the way Tim joins in everything?'

How they all worked! How they all longed to find the entrance to the underground dungeons! What a thrill that would be.

12 Exciting discoveries

Soon the stones of the little room were clear of earth, sand and weeds. The children saw that they were all the same size – big and square, fitted well together. They went over them carefully with their torches, trying to find one that might move or lift.

'We'll probably find one with an iron ring handle sunk into it,' said Julian. But they didn't. All the stones looked exactly the same. It was very disappointing.

Julian tried inserting his spade into the cracks between the various stones, to see if by any chance he could move one. But they couldn't be moved. It seemed as if they were all set in the solid ground. After about three hours' hard work the children sat down to eat a meal.

They were very hungry indeed, and felt glad that there were so many things to eat. As they ate they discussed the problem.

'It looks as if the entrance to the dungeons isn't under this little room after all,' said Julian. 'It's disappointing – but somehow I don't think now that the steps down to the dungeon started from here. Let's measure the map and see if we can make out exactly where the steps start. It may be that the measurements are wrong and won't be any help to us at all. But we can try.'

So they measured as best they could, to try and find out in exactly what place the dungeon steps seemed to begin. It was impossible to tell, for the plans of the three floors seemed to be done to different scales. Julian stared at the map, puzzled. It seemed hopeless. Surely they wouldn't have to hunt all over the ground floor of the castle! It would take ages.

'Look,' said George, suddenly, putting her finger on the hole that they all thought must be meant to represent the well. 'The entrance to the dungeons seems to be not very far from the well. If only we could find the well, we could hunt around a bit for the beginning of the dungeon steps. The well is shown in both maps. It seems to be somewhere about the middle of the castle.'

'That's a good idea,' said Julian. 'Let's go out

into the middle of the castle – we can more or less guess where the old well ought to be, because it definitely seems to be about the middle of the old yard out there.'

Out they all went into the sunshine. They felt very important and serious. It was exciting to be looking for lost ingots of gold. They all felt certain that they really were somewhere beneath their feet. It didn't occur to any of the children that the treasure might not be there.

They stood in the ruined courtyard that had once been the centre of the castle. They paced out the middle of the yard and then stood there, looking around in vain for anything that might be the opening of an old well. It was all so overgrown. Sand had blown in from the shore, and weeds and bushes of all kinds grew there. The stones that had once formed the floor of the big courtyard were now cracked and were no longer lying flat. Most of them were covered with sand or weeds.

'Look! There's a rabbit!' cried Dick, as a big sandy rabbit lolloped slowly across the yard. It disappeared into a hole on the other side. Then another rabbit appeared, sat up and looked at the children, and then vanished too. The children were thrilled. They had never seen such tame rabbits before.

A third rabbit appeared. It was a small one with absurdly big ears, and the tiniest white bob of a tail. It didn't even look at the children. It bounded about in a playful way, and then, to their huge delight, it sat up on its hind legs, and began to wash its big ears, pulling down first one and then the other.

But this was too much for Timothy. He had watched the other two bound across the yard and then disappear without so much as barking at them. But to see this youngster actually sitting there washing its ears under his very nose was really too much for any dog. He gave an excited yelp and rushed full-tilt at the surprised rabbit.

For a moment the little thing didn't move. It had never been frightened or chased before, and it stared with big eyes at the rushing dog. Then it turned around and tore off at top speed, its white bobtail going up and down as it bounded away. It disappeared under a gorse bush near the children. Timothy went after it, vanishing under the big bush too.

Then a shower of sand and earth was thrown

up as Tim tried to go down the hole after the rabbit and scraped and scrabbled with his strong front paws as fast as he could. He yelped and whined in excitement, not seeming to hear George's voice calling to him. He meant to get that rabbit! He went almost mad as he scraped at the hole, making it bigger and bigger.

'Tim! Do you hear me! Come out of there!' shouted George. 'You're not to chase the rabbits here. You know you mustn't. You're very naughty. Come out!'

But Tim didn't come out. He just went on and on scraping away madly. George went to fetch him. Just as she got up to the gorse bush the scraping suddenly stopped. There came a scared yelp – and no more noise was heard. George peered under the prickly bush in astonishment.

Tim had disappeared! He just simply wasn't there any more. There was the big rabbit-hole, made enormous by Tim – but there was no Tim.

'Julian – Tim's gone,' said George in a scared voice. 'He surely can't have gone down the rabbit's hole, can he? I mean – he's such a big dog!'

The children crowded round the big gorse bush.

They heard a muffled whine from somewhere below it. Julian looked astonished.

'He is down the hole!' he said. 'How strange! I never heard of a dog really going down a rabbit-hole before. How are we going to get him out?'

'We'll have to dig up the gorse bush, to begin with,' said George, in a determined voice. She would have dug up the whole of Kirrin Castle to get Tim back, that was certain! 'I can't have poor Tim whining for help down there and not do what we can to help him.'

The bush was far too big and prickly to creep underneath. Julian was glad they had brought tools of all kinds. He went to fetch an axe. They had brought a small one with them and it would do to chop away the prickly branches and trunk of the gorse bush. The children slashed at it and soon the poor bush began to look a sorry sight.

It took a long time to destroy it, for it was prickly, sturdy and stout. Everyone's hands were scratched by the time the bush had been reduced to a mere stump. Then they could see the hole quite well. Julian shone his torch down it.

He gave a shout of surprise. 'I know what's happened! The old well is here! The rabbits had a hole at the side of it – and Tim scraped away to make it bigger and uncovered a bit of the well-hole – and he's fallen down the well!'

'Oh no, oh no,' cried George, in panic. 'Oh Tim, Tim, are you all right?'

A distant whine came to their ears. Evidently Tim was there somewhere. The children looked at one another.

'Well, there's only one thing to do,' said Julian. 'We must get our spades now and dig out the hole of the well. Then maybe we can let a rope down or something and get Tim.'

They set to work with their spades. It wasn't really difficult to uncover the hole, which had been blocked only by the spreading roots of the big gorse bush, some fallen masonry, earth, sand and small stones. At some time a big slab had fallen from part of the tower across the well-hole, and partly closed it. The weather and the growing gorse bush had done the rest.

It took all the children together to move the slab. Underneath was a very rotten wooden cover, which had plainly been used in the old days to protect the well. It had rotted so much that when Tim's weight had been pressed on it, it had given just there and made a hole for Tim to fall through.

Julian removed the old wooden cover and then the children could see down the well-hole. It was very deep and very dark. They couldn't see the bottom. Julian took a stone and dropped it down. They all listened for the splash. But there was no splash. Either there was no longer any water there, or the well was too deep even to hear the splash!

'I think it's too deep for us to hear anything,' said Julian. 'Now – where's Tim?'

He shone his torch down – and there was Tim! Many years before a big slab had fallen down the well itself and had stuck a little way down, across the well-hole – and on this old cracked slab sat Tim, his big eyes staring up in fright. He couldn't understand what had happened to him.

There was an old iron ladder fastened to the side of the well. George was on it before anyone else could get there! Down she went, not caring if the ladder held or not, and reached Tim. Somehow she got him on to her shoulder and, holding him there with one hand, she climbed slowly up again. The other three hauled her out and Tim jumped round her, barking and licking for all he was worth!

'Well, Tim!' said Dick. 'You shouldn't chase rabbits – but you've done us a good turn, because you've found the well for us! Now we've only got to look around a little to find the dungeon entrance!'

They set to work again to hunt for the dungeon entrance. They dug about with their spades under all the bushes. They pulled up crooked stones and dug their spades into the earth below, hoping that they might suddenly find them going through into space! It was really thrilling.

And then Anne found the entrance! It was quite by accident. She was tired and sat down to rest. She lay on her front and scrabbled about in the sand. Suddenly her fingers touched something hard and cold. She brushed the sand away from it – and found an iron ring! She gave a shout and the others looked up.

'There's a stone with an iron ring in it here!' yelled Anne, excitedly. They all rushed over to her. Julian dug about with his spade and uncovered the whole stone. Sure enough, it did have a ring in it – and rings are only set into stones that need to be moved! Surely this stone must be the one that covered the dungeon entrance!

All the children took turns at pulling on the iron ring, but the stone did not move. Then Julian tied two or three turns of rope through it and the four children combined their full strength and pulled for all they were worth.

The stone moved. 'All together again!' cried Julian. And all together they pulled. The stone stirred again and then suddenly gave way. It moved upwards – and the children fell over on top of one another like a row of dominoes suddenly pushed down! Tim darted to the hole and barked madly down it as if all the rabbits of the world lived there!

Julian and George shot to their feet and rushed to the opening that the moved stone had uncovered. They stood there, looking downwards, their faces shining with delight. They had found the entrance to the dungeons! A steep flight of steps, cut out of the rock itself, led downwards into deep darkness.

'Come on!' cried Julian, snapping on his torch. 'We've found what we wanted! Now for the dungeons!'

The steps down were slippery. Tim darted down first, lost his footing and rolled down five or six steps, yelping with fright. Julian went after him, then George, then Dick and then Anne. They were all hugely excited. They almost expected to see piles of gold and all kinds of treasure everywhere around them!

It was dark down the steep flight of steps, and smelt very musty. Anne choked a little.

'I hope the air down here is all right,' said Julian. 'Sometimes it isn't good in these underground places. If anyone feels a bit funny they'd better say so and we'll go up into the open air again.'

But however funny they might feel, nobody would have said so. It was all far too exciting to worry about feeling strange.

The steps went down a long way. Then they came to an end. Julian stepped down from the last rock-stair and flashed his torch around. It was a weird sight that met his eyes.

The dungeons of Kirrin Castle were made out of the rock itself. Whether there were natural caves here, or whether they had been hollowed out by man the children could not tell. But certainly they were very mysterious, dark and full of echoing sounds. When Julian gave a sigh of excitement it fled into the rocky hollows and swelled out and echoed around as if it were a live thing. It gave all the children a very odd feeling.

'Isn't it strange?' said George, in a low voice. At once the echoes took up her words, and multiplied them and made them louder – and all the dungeon caves gave back the girl's words over and over again. 'Isn't it strange, ISN'T IT STRANGE, ISN'T IT STRANGE.'

Anne slipped her hand into Dick's. She felt scared. She didn't like the echoes at all. She knew they were only echoes – but they did sound exactly like the voices of dozens of people hidden in the caves!

'Where do you think the ingots are?' said Dick. And at once the caves threw back his words. INGOTS! INGOTS ARE! INGOTS ARE! ARE! ARE!

Julian laughed – and his laugh was split up into dozens of different laughs that came out of the dungeons and spun round the listening children. It sounded very strange.

'Come on,' said Julian. 'Maybe the echoes won't be so bad a little farther in.'

'FARTHER IN,' said the echoes at once. 'FARTHER IN!'

They moved away from the end of the rocky steps and explored the nearby dungeons. They were really only rocky cellars stretching under the castle. Maybe poor prisoners had been kept there many, many years before, but mostly they had been used for storing things.

'I wonder which dungeon was used for storing the ingots,' said Julian. He stopped and took the map out of his pocket. He flashed his torch on to it. But although it showed him quite plainly the dungeon where Ingots were marked, he had no idea at all of the right direction.

'Look – there's a door here, shutting off the next dungeon!' suddenly cried Dick. 'I bet this is the dungeon we're looking for! I bet there are ingots in here!'

13 Down in the dungeons

Four torches were flashed on to the wooden door.
It was big and stout, studded with great iron nails.
Julian gave a whoop of delight and rushed to it.
He felt certain that behind it was the dungeon
used for storing things.

But the door was fast shut. No amount of
pushing or pulling would open it. It had a great
keyhole – but no key there! The four children
stared in exasperation at the door. Bother it! Just
as they really thought they were near the ingots,
this door wouldn't open!

'Let's fetch the axe,' said Julian, suddenly.
'We may be able to chop round the keyhole and
smash the lock.'

'That's a good idea!' said George, delighted.
'Come on back!'

They left the big door, and tried to go back the
way they had come. But the dungeons were so big
and so rambling that they lost their way. They

stumbled over old broken barrels, rotting wood, empty bottles and many other things as they tried to find their way back to the big flight of rock-steps.

'This is sickening!' said Julian, at last. 'I haven't got a clue where the entrance is. We keep on going into one dungeon after another, and one passage after another, and they all look exactly the same – dark and smelly and mysterious.'

'What if we have to stay here all the rest of our lives?' said Anne, gloomily.

'Idiot!' said Dick, taking her hand. 'We'll soon find the way out. Here – what's this?'

They all stopped. They had come to what looked like a chimney shaft of brick, stretching down from the roof of the dungeon to the floor. Julian flashed his torch on to it. He was puzzled.

'I know what it is!' said George, suddenly. 'It's the well, of course! You remember it was shown in the plan of the dungeons, as well as in the plan of the ground floor. Well, that's the shaft of the well going down and down. I wonder if there's any opening in it just here – so that water could be taken into the dungeons as well as up to the ground floor.'

They went to see. On the other side of the well-shaft was a small opening big enough for one child at a time to put his head and shoulders through and look down. They shone their torches down and up. The well was so deep that it was still impossible to see the bottom of it. Julian dropped a stone down again, but there was no sound of either a thud or a splash. He looked upwards, and could see the faint gleam of daylight that slid round the broken slab of stone lying a little way down the shaft – the slab on which Tim had sat, waiting to be rescued.

'Yes,' he said, 'this is definitely the well. Isn't it weird? Now we've found the well we know that the entrance to the dungeons isn't very far off!'

That cheered them all up. They held hands and hunted around in the dark, their torches making bright beams of light here and there.

Anne gave a screech of excitement. 'Here's the entrance! It must be, because I can see faint daylight coming down!'

The children rounded a corner and sure enough, there was the steep, rocky flight of steps leading upwards. Julian took a quick look round, trying to remember the way to go when they came down again. He didn't feel at all certain that he'd find the wooden door!

They all went up into the sunshine. It was wonderful to feel the warmth on their heads and shoulders after the cold air down in the dungeons. Julian looked at his watch and gave a loud exclamation.

'It's half-past six! *Half-past six!* No wonder I feel hungry. We haven't had any tea. We've been working, and wandering about those dungeons for hours.'

'Well, let's have a kind of tea-supper before we do anything else,' said Dick. 'I don't feel as if I've had anything to eat for about twelve months.'

'Well, considering you ate about twice as much as anyone else at dinner-time,' began Julian, indignantly. Then he grinned. 'I feel the same as you,' he said. 'Come on! – let's get a really good meal. George, what about boiling a kettle and making some cocoa, or something? I feel cold after all that time underground.'

It was fun boiling the kettle on a fire of dry sticks. It was lovely to lie about in the warmth of the evening sun and munch bread and cheese and enjoy cake and biscuits. They all enjoyed themselves thoroughly. Tim had a good meal too. He hadn't liked being underground, and had followed the others very closely indeed, his tail well down. He had been very frightened, too, of the curious echoes here and there.

Once he had barked, and it had seemed to Tim as if the whole of the dungeons were full of other dogs, all barking far more loudly than he could. He hadn't even dared to whine after that! But now he was happy again, eating the tit-bits that the children gave him, and licking George whenever he was near her.

It was past eight o'clock by the time that the children had finished their meal and tidied up. Julian looked at the others. The sun was sinking, and the day was no longer so warm.

'Well,' he said, 'I don't know about you, but I don't really want to go down into those dungeons again today, not even for the sake of smashing in that door with the axe and opening it! I'm tired – and I don't like the thought of losing my way in those dungeons at night.'

The others thoroughly agreed with him, especially Anne, who had secretly been dreading going down again with the night coming on. The little girl was almost asleep; she was so tired out with hard work and excitement.

'Come on, Anne!' said George, pulling her to her feet. 'Bed for you. We'll cuddle up together in the rugs on the floor of that little room – and in the morning we'll have the excitement of opening that big wooden door.'

All four children, with Tim close behind, went off to the little stone room. They curled up on their piles of rugs, and Tim crept in with George and Anne. He lay down on them, and felt so heavy that Anne had to push him off her legs.

He sat himself down on her again, and she groaned, half-asleep. Tim wagged his tail and thumped it hard against her ankles. Then George pulled him on to her legs and lay there, feeling him breathe. She was very happy. She was spending the night on her island. They had almost found the ingots, she was sure. She had Tim with her, actually sleeping on her rugs. Perhaps everything would come right after all.

She fell asleep. The children felt completely safe with Tim on guard. They slept peacefully until the morning, when Tim saw a rabbit through the broken archway leading to the little room, and sped away to chase it. He awoke George as he got up from the rugs, and she sat up and rubbed her eyes.

'Wake up!' she cried to the others. 'Wake up, all of you! It's morning! And we're on the island!'

They all awoke. It was very exciting to sit up and remember everything. Julian thought of the big wooden door at once. He would soon smash it in with his axe, he felt sure. And then what would they find?

They had breakfast, and ate just as much as ever. Then Julian picked up the axe they had brought and took everyone to the flight of steps. Tim went too, wagging his tail, but not really feeling very pleased at the thought of going down into the strange places where other dogs seemed to bark, and yet were not to be found. Poor Tim would never understand echoes!

They all went down underground again. And then, of course, they couldn't find the way to the wooden door! It was really annoying.

'We'll lose our way all over again,' said George, desperately. 'These dungeons are the most rambling spread-out maze of underground caves I've ever known! We'll lose the entrance again too!'

Julian had a bright idea. He had a piece of white chalk in his pocket, and he took it out. He went back to the steps, and marked the wall there. Then he began to put chalk-marks along the passages as they walked in the musty darkness. They came to the well, and Julian was pleased.

'Now,' he said, 'whenever we come to the well we'll definitely be able to find the way back to the steps, because we can follow my chalk-marks. Now the thing is – which is the way next? We'll try and find it and I'll put chalk-marks along the walls here and there – but if we go the wrong way and have to come back, we'll rub out the marks, and start again from the well another way.'

This was a very good idea. They did go the wrong way, and had to come back, rubbing out Julian's marks. They reached the well, and set off in the opposite direction. And this time they found the wooden door!

There it was, stout and sturdy, its old iron nails rusty and red. The children stared at it in delight. Julian lifted his axe.

Crash! He drove it into the wood and round

about the keyhole. But the wood was still strong, and the axe only went in an inch or two. Julian drove it in once more. The axe hit one of the big nails and slipped a little to one side. A big splinter of wood flew out – and struck poor Dick on the cheek!

He gave a yell of pain. Julian jumped in alarm, and turned to look at him. Dick's cheek was pouring with blood!

'Something flew out of the door and hit me,' said Dick. 'It's a splinter, or something.'

'Oh no!' said Julian, and he shone his torch on to Dick. 'Can you bear it if I pull the splinter out? It's a big one, and it's still sticking into your cheek.'

But Dick pulled it out himself. He made a face with the pain, and then turned very white.

'You'd better get up into the open air for a bit,' said Julian. 'And we'll have to bathe your cheek and stop it bleeding somehow. Anne's got a clean hanky. We'll bathe it and dab it with that. We brought some water with us, luckily.'

'I'll go with Dick,' said Anne. 'You stay here with George. There's no need for us all to go.'

But Julian wanted to see Dick safely up into the

open air first, and then he could leave him with Anne while he went back to George and carried on with the smashing down of the door. He handed the axe to George.

'You can do a bit of chopping while I'm gone,' he said. 'It'll take a while to smash that big door in. You get on with it – and I'll be back down in a few minutes. We can easily find the way to the entrance because we've only got to follow my chalk-marks.'

'Right!' said George, and she took the axe. 'Poor Dick – you do look a sight.'

Leaving George behind with Tim, valiantly attacking the big door, Julian took Dick and Anne up to the open air. Anne dipped her hanky into the kettle of water and dabbed Dick's cheek gently. It was bleeding a lot, as cheeks do, but the wound wasn't really very bad. Dick's colour soon came back, and he wanted to go down into the dungeons again.

'No, you'd better lie down on your back for a while,' said Julian. 'That might be good for cheek-bleeding. Why don't you and Anne go out on the rocks over there, where you can see the wreck, and stay there for half an hour or so?

Come on – I'll take you both there, and leave you for a bit. You'd better not get up till your cheek's stopped bleeding.'

Julian took the two out of the castle yard and out on to the rocks on the side of the island that faced the open sea. The dark hulk of the old wreck was still there on the rocks. Dick lay down on his back and stared up into the sky, hoping that his cheek would soon stop bleeding. He didn't want to miss any of the fun!

Anne took his hand. She was very upset at the little accident, and although she didn't want to miss the fun either, she meant to stay with Dick till he felt better. Julian sat down beside them for a minute or two. Then he went back to the rocky steps and disappeared down them. He followed his chalk-marks, and soon came to where George was attacking the door.

She had smashed it well round the lock – but it simply would *not* give way. Julian took the axe from her and drove it hard into the wood.

After a blow or two something seemed to happen to the lock. It became loose, and hung a little sideways. Julian put down his axe.

'I think somehow that we can open the door

now,' he said, in an excited voice. 'Get out of the way, Tim, old fellow. Now then, push, George!'

They both pushed – and the lock gave way with a grating noise. The big door opened creakingly, and the two children went inside, flashing their torches around in excitement.

The room wasn't much more than a cave, hollowed out of the rock – but in it was something very different from the old barrels and boxes the children had found before. At the back, in untidy piles, were curious, brick-shaped things of dull yellow-brown metal. Julian picked one up.

'George!' he cried. 'The ingots! These are real gold! I know they don't look like it – but they are. George, there's a small fortune here in this cellar – and it's yours! We've found it at last!'

14 Prisoners!

George couldn't say a word. She just stood there, staring at the pile of ingots, holding one in her hand. She could hardly believe that these strange brick-shaped things were really gold. Her heart thumped fast. What a wonderful, incredible discovery!

Suddenly Tim began to bark loudly. He stood with his back to the children, his nose towards the door – and he barked like mad!

'Shut up, Tim!' said Julian. 'What can you hear? Is it the others coming back?'

He went to the door and yelled down the passage outside. 'Dick! Anne! Is it you? Come quickly, because we've found the ingots! We've found them! Quick! Hurry!'

Tim stopped barking and began to growl. George looked puzzled. 'What *can* be the matter with Tim?' she said. 'He surely can't be growling at Dick and Anne.'

Then both children got a huge shock – for a man's voice came booming down the dark passage, making strange echoes all around.

'Who is here? Who is down here?'

George clutched Julian in fright. Tim went on growling, all the hairs on his neck standing up straight. 'Be quiet, Tim!' whispered George, snapping off her torch. But Tim would not be quiet. He went on growling as if he were a small thunderstorm.

The children saw the beam of a powerful torchlight coming round the corner of the dungeon passage. Then the light picked them out, and the holder of the torch came to a surprised stop.

'Well, well, well!' said a voice. 'Look who's here! Two children in the dungeons of my castle.'

'What do you mean, *your* castle!' cried George.

'Well, my dear little girl, it *is* my castle, because I'm in the process of buying it,' said the voice. Then another voice spoke, more gruffly.

'What are you doing down here? What did you mean when you shouted out "Dick" and "Anne", and said you had found the ingots? What ingots?'

'Don't answer,' whispered Julian to George.

But the echoes took his words and made them very loud in the passage. 'DON'T ANSWER! DON'T ANSWER!'

'Oh, so you won't answer,' said the second man, and he stepped towards the children. Tim bared his teeth, but the man didn't seem at all frightened of him. The man went to the door and flashed his torch inside the dungeon. He gave a long whistle of surprise.

'Jake! Look here!' he said. 'You were right. The gold's here all right. And how easy to take away! All in ingots! This is the most amazing thing we've ever found.'

'This gold is mine,' said George, in a fury. 'This island and the castle belong to my mum – and so does anything found here. This gold was brought here and stored by my great-great-great-grandfather before his ship got wrecked. It's not yours, and never will be. As soon as I get back home I'm going to tell my parents what we've found – and then you won't be able to buy the castle or the island! You were very clever, finding out from the map in the old box about the gold – but just not clever enough to beat us. We found it first!'

The men listened in silence to George's clear and angry voice. One of them laughed. 'You're only a kid,' he said. 'You surely don't think you can keep us from getting our way? We're going to buy this island – and everything in it – and we shall take the gold when the deeds are signed. And if by any chance we can't buy the island, we'll take the gold just the same. It'd be easy enough to bring a ship here and transfer the ingots from here by boat to the ship. Don't worry – we shall get what we want all right.'

'You will not!' said George, and she stepped out of the door. 'I'm going straight home now – and I'll tell my dad exactly what you've said.'

'My dear little girl, you are not going home,' said the first man, putting his hands on George's shoulders and forcing her back into the dungeon. 'And, by the way, unless you want me to shoot this unpleasant dog of yours, call him off, will you?'

George saw, to her horror, that the man had a shining revolver in his hand. In fright she caught hold of Tim's collar and pulled him to her. 'Be quiet, Tim,' she said. 'It's all right.'

But Tim knew that it wasn't all right. Something

was very wrong. He went on growling fiercely.

'Now listen to me,' said the man, after he had had a hurried talk with his companion. 'If you're sensible, nothing unpleasant will happen to you. But if you want to be obstinate, you'll be very sorry. What we are going to do is this – we're going off in our motor-boat, leaving you nicely locked up here – and we're going to get a ship and come back for the gold. There's no point buying the island now we know where the ingots are.'

'And you're going to write a note to your friends above, telling them you've found the gold and they are to come down and see it,' said the other man. 'Then we shall lock up all of you in this dungeon, with the ingots to play with, leaving you food and drink till we come back. Here's a pencil. Write a note to Dick and Anne, whoever they are, and send your dog up with it. Come on.'

'I won't,' said George, her face furious. 'I won't. You can't make me do a thing like that. I won't get poor Dick and Anne down here to be made prisoners. And I won't let you have my gold, just when I've discovered it.'

'We'll shoot your dog if you don't do as you're

told,' said the first man, suddenly. George's heart sank down and she felt cold and terrified.

'No, no,' she said in a low, desperate voice.

'Well, write the note then,' said the man, offering her a pencil and paper. 'Go on. I'll tell you what to say.'

'I can't!' sobbed George. 'I don't want to get Dick and Anne down here to be made prisoners.'

'All right – I'll shoot the dog then,' said the man in a cold voice, and he aimed his revolver at poor Tim. George threw her arms round her dog and gave a scream.

'No, no! I'll write the note. Don't shoot Tim, don't shoot him!'

She took the paper and pencil in a shaking hand and looked at the man. 'Write this,' he ordered. ' "Dear Dick and Anne. We've found the gold. Come on down at once and see it." Then sign your name, whatever it is.'

George wrote what the man had said. Then she signed her name. But instead of writing 'George' she put 'Georgina'. She hoped that the others would know she would never sign herself that – and that it would warn them that something was wrong. The man took the note and fastened it to

Tim's collar. The dog growled all the time, but George kept telling him not to bite.

'Now tell him to go and find your friends,' said the man.

'Find Dick and Anne,' commanded George. 'Go on, Tim. Find Dick and Anne. Give them the note.'

Tim did not want to leave George, but there was something very urgent in her voice. He took one last look at his mistress, gave her hand a lick and sped off down the passage. He knew the way now. Up the rocky steps he bounded and into the open air. He stopped in the old yard, sniffing. Where were Dick and Anne?

He smelt their footsteps and ran off, his nose to the ground. He soon found the two children out on the rocks. Dick was feeling better now and was sitting up. His cheek had almost stopped bleeding.

'Hey,' he said in surprise, when he saw Tim. 'Here's Timothy! Tim, why have you come to see us? Did you get tired of being underground in the dark?'

'Look, Dick – he's got something twisted into his collar,' said Anne, her sharp eyes seeing the paper there. 'It's a note. I expect it's from the others, telling us to go down. Isn't Tim clever to bring it?'

Dick took the paper from Tim's collar. He undid it and read it.

' "Dear Dick and Anne," ' he read out aloud. ' "We've found the gold. Come on down at once and see it. Georgina." '

'Ooooh!' said Anne, her eyes shining. 'They've found it. Dick – are you well enough to come now? Let's hurry.'

But Dick did not get up from the rocks. He sat and stared at the note, puzzled.

'What's the matter?' said Anne, impatiently.

'Well, don't you think it's funny that George should suddenly sign herself "Georgina"?' said Dick, slowly. 'You know how she hates being a girl, and having a girl's name. You know she'll never answer if anyone calls her Georgina. And yet in this note she signs herself by the name she hates. It seems a bit funny to me. Almost as if it's a kind of warning that there's something wrong.'

'Oh, don't be so silly, Dick,' said Anne. 'What could be wrong? Come on.'

'Anne, I'd like to pop over to that inlet of ours

to make sure there's no one else on the island,' said Dick. 'You stay here.'

But Anne didn't want to stay there alone. She ran round the coast with Dick, telling him all the time that she thought he was very silly.

But when they came to the little harbour, they saw that there was another boat there, as well as their own. It was a motor-boat! Someone else was on the island!

'Look,' said Dick, in a whisper. 'There is someone else here. And I bet it's the men who want to buy the island. I bet they've read that old map and know there's gold here. And they've found George and Julian and want to get us all together down in the dungeons so that they can keep us safe till they've stolen the gold. That's why they made George send us that note – but she signed it with a name she never uses – to warn us! We have to think hard. What are we going to do?'

15 Dick to the rescue!

Dick grabbed Anne's hand and pulled her quickly away from the cove. He was afraid that whoever had come to the island might be somewhere nearby and see them. He led Anne to the little stone room where their things were and they sat down in a corner.

'Whoever has come must have discovered Julian and George smashing in that door,' said Dick, in a whisper. 'I can't think what to do. We mustn't go down into the dungeons or we'll be caught. Hey – where's Tim off to?'

The dog had stayed with them for a while but now he ran off to the entrance of the dungeons. He disappeared down the steps. He wanted to get back to George, because he knew she was in danger. Dick and Anne stared after him. They had felt comforted while he was there, and now they were sorry he had gone.

They really didn't know what to do. Then Anne

had an idea. 'I know!' she said. 'We'll row back to the land in our boat and get help.'

'I'd thought of that,' said Dick, gloomily. 'But we'd never know the way in and out of those awful rocks. We'd wreck the boat. I'm sure we're not strong enough either to row all the way back. I wish we could think what to do.'

They didn't need to puzzle their brains long. The men came up out of the dungeons and began to hunt for them! They had seen Tim when he came back and had found the note gone. So they knew the two children had taken it – and they couldn't imagine why they had not obeyed what George had said in the note, and come down to the dungeons!

Dick heard their voices. He clutched hold of Anne to make her keep quiet. He saw through the broken archway that the men were going in the opposite direction.

'Anne! I know where we can hide!' said the boy, excitedly. 'Down the old well! We can climb down the ladder a little way and hide there. I'm sure no one would ever look there!'

Anne didn't want to climb down the well even a little way. But Dick pulled her to her feet and hurried her off to the middle of the old courtyard. The men were hunting around the other side of the castle. There was just time to climb in. Dick slipped aside the old wooden cover of the well and helped Anne down the ladder. She was very scared. Then Dick climbed down himself and slipped the wooden cover back again over his head, as best he could.

The old stone slab that Tim had sat on when he fell down the well was still there. Dick climbed down to it and tested it. It was immovable.

'It's safe for you to sit on, Anne, if you don't want to keep clinging to the ladder,' he whispered. So Anne sat shivering on the stone slab across the well-shaft, waiting to see if they were discovered or not. They kept hearing the voices of the men, now close by and now far-off. Then the men began to shout for them.

'Dick! Anne! The others want you! Where are you? We've got some exciting news for you.'

'Well, why don't they let Julian and George come up and tell us then?' whispered Dick. 'There's something wrong, I know there is. I wish we could get to Julian and George and find out what's happened.'

The two men came into the courtyard. They were angry. 'Where have those kids got to?' said Jake. 'Their boat is still in the cove, so they haven't got away. They must be hiding somewhere. We can't wait all day for them.'

'Let's take some food and drink down to the two we've locked up,' said the other man. 'There's plenty in that little stone room. I suppose it's a store the children brought over. We'll leave half in the room so that the other two kids can have it. And we'll take their boat with us so that they can't escape.'

'Right,' said Jake. 'The thing to do is to get the gold away as quickly as possible, and make sure the children are prisoners here until we've made a safe getaway. We won't bother any more about trying to buy the island. After all, it was only the thought of getting the ingots that put us up to the idea of getting Kirrin Castle and the island.'

'Come on,' said his companion. 'We'll take the food down now, and not bother about the other kids. You stay here and see if you can spot them while I go down.'

Dick and Anne hardly dared to breathe when

they heard all this. They hoped that the men wouldn't think of looking down the well! They heard one man walk to the little stone room. It was plain that he was getting food and drink to take down to the two prisoners in the dungeons below. The other man stayed in the courtyard, whistling softly.

After what seemed a very long time to the hidden children, the first man came back. Then the two talked together, and at last went off to the cove. Dick heard the motor-boat being started up.

'It's safe to get out now, Anne,' he said. 'Isn't it cold down here? I'll be glad to get out into the sunshine.'

They climbed out and stood warming themselves in the hot summer sunshine. They could see the motor-boat streaking towards the mainland.

'Well, they're gone for the moment,' said Dick. 'And they haven't taken our boat, as they said. If only we could rescue Julian and George, we could get help, because George could row us back.'

'Why can't we rescue them?' cried Anne, her eyes shining. 'We can go down the steps and unbolt the door, can't we?'

'No – we can't,' said Dick. 'Look!'

Anne looked to where he pointed. She saw that the two men had piled big, heavy slabs of broken stone over the dungeon entrance. It had taken all their strength to put the big stones there. Neither Dick nor Anne could hope to move them.

'It's impossible to get down the steps,' said Dick. 'They've made sure we can't do that! And we have no idea where the second entrance is. We only know it was somewhere near the tower.'

'Let's see if we can find it,' said Anne eagerly. They set off to the tower on the right of the castle – but whatever entrance there might have been once, it was gone now! The castle had fallen in very much just there, and there were piles of old broken stones everywhere, completely impossible to move. The children soon gave up the search.

'This is terrible!' said Dick. 'Julian and George are prisoners down there, and we can't even help them! Oh, Anne – can't *you* think of something to do?'

Anne sat down on a stone and thought hard. She was very worried. Then she brightened up a little and turned to Dick.

'Dick! I suppose – I suppose we couldn't

possibly climb down the well, could we?' she asked. 'You know it goes past the dungeons – and there's an opening on the dungeon floor from the well-shaft, because we were able to put in our heads and shoulders and look right up the well to the top. Could we get past that slab, do you think – the one that I sat on just now, that has fallen across the well?'

Dick thought it all over. He went to the well and peered down it. 'You know, I think you're right, Anne,' he said at last. 'We might be able to squeeze past that slab. There's just about room. I don't know how far the iron ladder goes down though.'

'Let's try,' said Anne. 'It's our only chance of rescuing the others!'

'OK,' said Dick, 'I'll try it – but not you, Anne. I don't want you falling down that well. The ladder might be broken half-way down – anything could happen. You'd better stay up here and I'll see what I can do.'

'You will be careful, won't you?' said Anne, anxiously. 'Take a rope with you, Dick, so that if you need one you won't have to climb all the way up again.'

'Good idea,' said Dick. He went to the little stone room and got one of the ropes they had put there. He wound it round and round his waist. Then he went back to Anne.

'Here goes!' he said, in a cheerful voice. 'Don't worry about me. I'll be all right.'

Anne was rather white. She was terrified that Dick might fall right down to the bottom of the well. She watched him climb down the iron ladder to the slab of stone. He tried his best to squeeze past it, but it was very difficult. At last he managed it and after that Anne couldn't see him. But she could hear him, because he kept calling up to her.

'Ladder's still going strong, Anne! I'm all right. Can you hear me?'

'Yes,' shouted Anne down the well, hearing her voice echo in a funny hollow way. 'Be careful, Dick. Does the ladder go all the way down?'

'I think it does!' yelled back Dick. Then he gave a loud exclamation. 'Oh no! It's broken just here. Broken right off. Or else it ends. I'll have to use my rope.'

There was a silence as Dick unwound the rope from his waist. He tied it firmly to the last but one rung of the ladder, which seemed quite strong.

'I'm going down the rope now!' he shouted to Anne. 'Don't worry. I'm all right. Here I go!'

Anne couldn't hear what Dick said after that, because the well-shaft made his words go crooked and she couldn't make out what they were. But she was glad to hear him shouting even though she didn't know what he was saying. She yelled down to him too, hoping he could hear her.

Dick slid down the rope, holding on to it with hands, knees and feet, glad that he was so good at gym at school. He wondered if he was anywhere near the dungeons. He seemed to have gone down a long way. He managed to get out his torch. He put it between his teeth after he had switched it on, so that he could have both hands free for the rope. The light from the torch showed him the walls of the well around him. He couldn't make out if he was above or below the dungeons. He didn't want to go right down to the bottom of the well!

He decided that he must have just passed the opening into the dungeon-caves. He climbed back up the rope a little way and to his delight saw the opening on to the dungeons just by his head. He climbed up till he was level with it and then swung himself to the side of the well where the small opening was. He managed to get hold of the bricked edge, and then tried to scramble through the opening into the dungeon.

It was difficult, but luckily Dick wasn't very big. He managed it at last and stood up straight with a sigh of relief. He was in the dungeons! He could now follow the chalk-marks to the room or cave where the ingots were – and where he felt sure that George and Julian were imprisoned!

He shone his torch on the wall. Yes – there were the chalk-marks. Good! He put his head into the well-opening and yelled at the top of his voice.

'Anne! I'm in the dungeons! Watch out that the men don't come back!'

Then he began to follow the white chalk-marks, his heart beating fast. After a while he came to the door of the store-room. As he had expected, it was fastened so that George and Julian couldn't get out. Big bolts had been driven home at the top and bottom, and the children inside could not possibly get out. They had tried their hardest to batter down the door, but it was no good at all.

They were sitting inside the store-cave, feeling angry and exhausted. The man had brought them food and drink, but they had not touched it. Tim was with them, lying down with his head on his paws, half-angry with George because she hadn't let him fly at the men as he had so badly wanted to. But George felt certain that Tim would be shot if he tried biting or snapping.

'Anyway, the other two had sense enough not to come down and be made prisoners too,' said George. 'They must have known there was something funny about that note when they saw I had signed myself Georgina instead of George. I wonder what they're doing. They must be hiding.'

Tim suddenly gave a growl. He leapt to his feet and went to the closed door, his head on one side. He had heard something.

'I hope it's not those men back again already,' said George. Then she looked at Tim in surprise, flashing her torch on to him. He was wagging his tail!

A great bang at the door made them all jump

out of their skins! Then came Dick's cheerful voice. 'Julian! George! Are you in there?'

'Wufffff!' barked Tim joyfully, and scratched at the door.

'Dick! Open the door!' yelled Julian in delight. 'Quick, open the door!'

16 A plan – and a narrow escape

Dick unbolted the door at the top and bottom and flung it open. He rushed in and thumped George and Julian happily on the back.

'Hello!' he said. 'How does it feel to be rescued?'

'Brilliant!' cried Julian, and Tim barked madly round them.

George grinned at Dick.

'Good work!' she said. 'What happened?'

Dick told them in a few words all that had happened. When he related how he had climbed down the old well, George and Julian could hardly believe their ears. Julian put his arm around his younger brother's shoulders.

'You're a hero!' he said. 'A real hero! Now quick – what are we going to do?'

'If they've left us our boat I'm going to take us all back to the mainland as fast as possible,' said

George. 'I'm not playing about with men who carry revolvers. Come on! Let's go up the well and find the boat.'

They ran to the well-shaft and squeezed through the small opening one by one. They climbed up the rope and soon found the iron ladder. Julian made them go up one by one in case the ladder wouldn't bear the weight of all three at once.

Soon they were all up in the open air once more, giving Anne hugs, and hearing her say, with tears in her eyes, how pleased she was to see them all again.

'Come on!' said George after a minute. 'Off to the boat. Quick! Those men may be back at any time.'

They rushed to the cove. There was their boat, lying where they had pulled it, out of reach of the waves. But then they had a terrible shock!

'They've taken the oars!' said George, in dismay. 'They know we can't row the boat away without oars. They were afraid you and Anne might row off, Dick – so instead of bothering to tow the boat behind them, they just grabbed the oars. Now we're stuck. We can't get away.'

It was a terrible blow. The children were almost

ready to cry. After Dick's wonderful rescue of George and Julian, it had seemed as if everything was going right – and now suddenly things were going wrong again.

'Let's think this through logically,' said Julian, sitting down where he could see at once if any boat came in sight. 'The men have gone off – probably to get a ship to take the ingots away. They won't be back for a while, I should think, because you can't charter a ship that fast – unless, of course, they've got one of their own.'

'And in the meantime we can't get off the island to get help, because they've got our oars,' said George. 'We can't even signal to any passing fishing-boat because they won't be out at the moment. The tide's wrong. It seems as if all we can do is wait here patiently till the men come back and take my gold! And we can't stop them.'

'You know – I've got a sort of plan coming into my head,' said Julian, slowly. 'Wait a bit – don't interrupt me. I'm thinking.'

The others waited in silence while Julian sat and frowned, thinking hard. Then he looked at the others with a smile.

'I think it'll work,' he said. 'Listen! We'll wait here till the men come back. What will they do? They'll drag away those stones at the top of the dungeon entrance, and go down the steps. They'll go to the store-room, where they left us – thinking we are still there – and they'll go into the room. But what if one of us is hidden down there ready to bolt them into the room? Then we can either go off in their motor-boat or our own boat if they bring back our oars – and get help.'

Anne thought it was a wonderful idea. But Dick and George did not look so certain. 'We'd have to go down and bolt that door again to make it seem as if we're still prisoners there,' said George. 'And what if the one who hides down there doesn't manage to bolt the men in? It might be hard to do that fast enough. Then they'll catch whoever we plan to leave down there – and come up to look for the rest of us.'

'That's true,' said Julian, thoughtfully. 'Well … say that Dick – or whoever goes down – doesn't manage to bolt them in and make them prisoners, and the men come up here again. All right – while they are down below we'll pile big stones over the entrance, just as they did. Then they won't be able to get out.'

'What about Dick down below?' said Anne, at once.

'I could climb up the well again!' said Dick, eagerly. 'I'll be the one to go down and hide. I'll do my best to bolt the men into the room. And if I have to escape I'll climb up the well-shaft again. The men don't know about that. So even if they're not prisoners in the dungeon room, they'll be prisoners underground!'

The children talked the plan over, and decided that it was the best they could think of. Then George said she thought it would be a good thing to have a meal. They were all half-starved and, now that the worry and excitement of being rescued was over, they were feeling very hungry!

They fetched some food from the little room and ate it in the cove, keeping a sharp look-out for the return of the men. After about two hours they saw a big fishing-boat appear in the distance, and heard the chug-chug-chug of a motor-boat, too.

'There they are!' said Julian, in excitement, and he jumped to his feet. 'That's the boat they plan to load with the ingots, and sail away in safety – and there's the motor-boat bringing the men back! Quick, Dick, go down the well and hide until you hear them in the dungeons!'

Dick shot off. Julian turned to the others. 'We'll have to hide,' he said. 'Now that the tide is out we'll hide over there, behind those uncovered rocks. I don't think the men will do any hunting for Dick and Anne – but they might. Come on! Quick!'

They all hid themselves behind the rocks, and heard the motor-boat come chugging into the tiny harbour. They could hear men calling to one another. It sounded as if there were more than two men this time. Then the men left the inlet and went up the low cliff towards the ruined castle.

Julian peered around the rocks to see what the men were doing. He felt certain they were pulling away the slabs of stone that had been piled on top of the entrance to stop Dick and Anne going down to rescue the others.

' Come on!' called Julian in a low tone. 'I think the men have gone down the steps into the dungeons now. We have to try to put those big stones back. Quick!'

George, Julian and Anne ran softly and swiftly to the old courtyard of the castle. They saw that the stones had been pulled away from the entrance to the dungeons. The men had disappeared. They had obviously gone down the steps.

The three children did their best to drag the heavy stones across the entrance. But they were not as strong as the men, and they couldn't manage to get any very big stones across. They put three smaller ones in place, and Julian hoped the men would find them too difficult to move from below. 'I just hope Dick has managed to bolt them into that room!' he said to the others. 'Come on, back to the well now. Dick will have to come up there, because he won't be able to get out of the entrance.'

They all went to the well. Dick had removed the old wooden cover, and it was lying on the ground. The children leaned over the hole of the well and waited anxiously. What was Dick doing? They could hear nothing from the well and they longed to know what was happening.

There was plenty happening down below! The two men, and another, had gone down into the dungeons, expecting, of course, to find

Julian, George and the dog still locked up in the store-room with the ingots. They passed the well-shaft not guessing that a boy was hidden there, ready to slip out of the opening as soon as they had passed.

Dick heard them pass. He slipped out of the well-opening and followed behind quietly, his feet making no sound. He could see the beams made by the men's powerful torches, and with his heart thumping loudly he crept along the smelly old passages, between great caves, until the men turned into the wide passage where the store-cave lay.

'Here it is,' Dick heard one of the men say, as he flashed his torch on to the great door. 'The gold's in there – so are the kids!'

The men unbolted the door at top and bottom. Dick was glad that he had slipped along to bolt the door, for if he hadn't done that before the men had come they would have known that Julian and George had escaped, and would have been on their guard.

The man opened the door and stepped inside. The second man followed him. Dick crept as close as he dared, waiting for the third man to go in too. Then he meant to slam the door and bolt it!

The first man swung his torch round and gave a loud exclamation. 'The children are gone! Where are they?'

Two of the men were now in the cave – and the third stepped in at that moment. Dick darted forward and slammed the door. It made a crash that went echoing round and round the caves and passages. Dick fumbled with the bolts, his hand trembling. They were stiff and rusty. The boy found it hard to shoot them home in their sockets. And meanwhile the men were not standing still!

As soon as they heard the door slam they spun round. The third man put his shoulder to the door at once and heaved hard. Dick had just got one of the bolts almost into its socket. Then all three men forced their strength against the door, and the bolt gave way!

Dick stared in horror. The door was opening! He turned and fled down the dark passage. The men flashed their torches on and saw him. They went after the boy at top speed.

Dick fled to the well-shaft. Luckily the opening was on the opposite side, and he could clamber into it without being seen in the light of the torches. The boy only just had time to squeeze through into the shaft before the three men came running by. Not one of them guessed that the runaway was squeezed into the well-shaft they passed! They didn't even know that there was a well there.

Trembling from head to foot, Dick began to climb the rope he had left dangling from the rungs of the iron ladder. He undid it as soon as he reached the ladder itself, because he thought that the men might discover the old well and try to climb up later. They would not be able to do that if there was no rope dangling down.

The boy climbed up the ladder quickly, and squeezed round the stone slab near the top. The other children were there, waiting for him.

They knew at once by the look on Dick's face that he had failed in what he had tried to do. They pulled him out quickly. 'It was no good,' said Dick, panting with his climb. 'I couldn't do it. They burst the door open just as I was bolting it, and chased me. I got into the shaft just in time.'

'They're trying to get out of the entrance now!' cried Anne, suddenly. 'Quick! What shall we do? They'll catch us all!'

'To the boat!' shouted Julian, grabbing Anne's hand to help her along. 'Come on! It's our only chance. The men might be able to move those stones.'

The four children fled down the courtyard. George darted into the little stone room as they passed it, and grabbed an axe. Dick wondered why she bothered to do that. Tim dashed along with them, barking madly.

They came to the cove. Their own boat lay there without oars. The motor-boat was there too. George jumped into it and gave a yell of delight.

'Here are our oars!' she shouted. 'Take them, Julian, I've got a job to do here! Get the boat down to the water, quick!'

Julian and Dick took the oars. Then they dragged their boat down to the water, wondering what George was doing. All kinds of crashing sounds were coming from the motor-boat!

'George! George! Hurry up. The men are out!' suddenly yelled Julian. He had seen the three men running to the cliff that led down to the cove. George leapt out of the motor-boat and joined the others. They pushed their boat out on to the water, and George took the oars at once, pulling for all she was worth.

The three men ran to their motor-boat. Then they stopped in shock – George had completely ruined it! She had chopped wildly with her axe at all the machinery she could see – and now the boat could not possibly be started! It was damaged beyond any repair the men could make with the few tools they had.

'You horrible little girl!' yelled Jake, shaking his fist at George. 'Wait till I get you!'

'I'll wait!' shouted back George, her blue eyes shining dangerously. 'And you can wait too! You won't be able to leave my island now!'

17 The end of the great adventure

The three men stood at the edge of the sea, watching George pull away strongly from the shore. They could do nothing. Their boat was quite useless.

'The fishing-boat they've got waiting out there is too big to use in that little inlet,' said George, as she pulled hard at her oars. 'They'll have to stay there till someone goes in with a boat. I bet they're furious!'

Their boat had to pass fairly near to the big fishing-boat. A man called to them as they came by.

'Ahoy there! Have you come from Kirrin Island?'

'Don't answer,' said George. 'Don't say a word.' So no one said anything at all, but looked the other way as if they hadn't heard.

'Ahoy there!' yelled the man, angrily. 'Are you deaf? Have you come from the island?'

Still the children said nothing at all, but looked away while George rowed steadily. The man on the ship gave up, and looked in a worried manner towards the island. He felt sure the children had come from there – and he knew enough of his comrades' adventures to wonder if everything was right on the island.

'He may put out a dinghy from the boat and go and see what's happening,' said George. 'Well, he can't do much except take the men away – with a few ingots! I don't think they'll dare to take any of the gold though, now that we've escaped to tell our tale!'

Julian looked behind at the ship. He saw after a time that the little dinghy it carried was being lowered into the sea. 'You're right,' he said to George. 'They've guessed something's wrong. They're going to rescue those three men. What a pity!'

Their little boat reached land. The children leapt out into the shallow water and dragged it up to the beach. Tim pulled at the rope too, wagging his tail. He loved to join in anything that the children were doing.

'Are you going to take Tim to Alf?' asked Dick.

George shook her head. 'No,' she said, 'we haven't any time to waste. We must go and tell everything that has happened. I'll tie Tim up to the fence in the front garden.'

They made their way to Kirrin Cottage at top speed. Aunt Fanny was gardening there. She stared in surprise at the hurrying children.

'Hello!' she said. 'I thought you weren't coming back till tomorrow or the next day! Has anything happened? What's the matter with Dick's cheek?'

'Nothing much,' said Dick.

The others chimed in.

'Aunt Fanny, where's Uncle Quentin? We've got something important to tell him!'

'Mum, we've had an amazing adventure!'

'Aunt Fanny, we've got so much to tell you! We really have!'

Aunt Fanny looked at the untidy children in amazement. 'What on earth has happened?' she said. Then she turned towards the house and called 'Quentin! Quentin! The children have something to tell us!'

Uncle Quentin came out, looking rather cross, because he was in the middle of his work. 'What's the matter?' he asked.

'Uncle, it's about Kirrin Island,' said Julian, eagerly. 'Those men haven't bought it yet, have they?'

'Well, it's almost sold,' said his uncle. 'I've signed my part, and they're going to sign their part tomorrow. Why?'

'Uncle, those men won't sign tomorrow,' said Julian. 'Do you know why they wanted to buy the island and the castle? Not because they really wanted to build an hotel or anything like that – but because they knew the lost gold was hidden there!'

'What nonsense are you talking?' said his uncle.

'It isn't nonsense, Dad!' cried George indignantly. 'It's all true. The map of the old castle was in that box you sold – and the map showed where the ingots were hidden by my great-great-great-grandfather!'

George's father looked amazed and annoyed. He simply didn't believe a word! But his wife could tell from the solemn and serious faces of the four children that something really important had happened. And then Anne suddenly burst into loud sobs! The excitement had been too much for her and she couldn't bear to think that her uncle wouldn't believe that everything was true.

'Aunt Fanny, it's all true!' she sobbed. 'Uncle Quentin *has* to believe us. Oh, Aunt Fanny, the man had a revolver – and he made Julian and George prisoners in the dungeons – and Dick had to climb down the well to rescue them. And George has smashed up their motor-boat to stop them escaping!'

Her aunt and uncle couldn't make head or tail of this, but Uncle Quentin suddenly seemed to think that the matter was serious and worth looking into. 'Smashed up a motor-boat!' he said. 'Whatever for? Come indoors. I'll have to hear the story from beginning to end. It seems quite unbelievable to me.'

They all trooped indoors. Anne sat on her aunt's knee and listened to George and Julian telling the whole story. They told it well and left nothing out. Aunt Fanny grew quite pale as she listened, especially when she heard about Dick climbing down the well.

'You could have been killed,' she said. 'Oh, Dick! What a brave thing to do!'

Uncle Quentin listened in amazement. He had

never had much liking or admiration for children – he always thought they were noisy, tiresome, and silly. But now, as he listened to Julian's tale, he changed his mind about these four children at once!

'You've been very clever,' he said. 'And very brave too. I'm proud of you. Yes, I'm very proud of you all. No wonder you didn't want me to sell the island, George, when you knew about the ingots! But why didn't you tell me?'

The four children stared at him and didn't answer. They couldn't very well say, 'Well, firstly, you wouldn't have believed us. Secondly, you're bad-tempered and unfair and we're scared of you. Thirdly, we didn't trust you enough to do the right thing.'

'Why don't you answer?' said their uncle. His wife answered for them, in a gentle voice.

'Quentin, you scare the children, you know, and I don't expect they liked to go to you. But now that they have, you'll be able to take matters into your own hands. The children can't do any more. You'll have to ring up the police and see what they have to say about all this.'

'Right,' said Uncle Quentin, and he got up at

once. He patted Julian on the back. 'You've all done well,' he said. Then he ruffled George's short curly hair. 'And I'm proud of you, too, George,' he said.

'Oh, Dad!' said George, going red with surprise and pleasure. She smiled at him and he smiled back. The children noticed that he had a very nice face when he smiled. He and George were really very similar. Both looked ugly when they sulked and frowned – and both were good looking when they laughed or smiled!

George's father went off to phone the police and his lawyer. The children sat and ate biscuits and plums, telling their aunt all the little details they had forgotten when telling the story before.

As they sat there, they heard a loud and angry bark from the front garden. George looked up. 'That's Tim,' she said, with an anxious glance at her mother. 'I didn't have time to take him to Alf, who keeps him for me. Mum, Tim was such a comfort to us on the island, you know. I'm sorry he's barking now – but I expect he's hungry.'

'Well, bring him in,' said her mother, unexpectedly. 'He's quite a hero, too – he deserves a good dinner.'

George smiled in delight. She sped out of the door and went to Tim. She set him free and he came bounding indoors, wagging his long tail. He licked George's mother and cocked his ears at her.

'Good dog,' she said, and actually patted him. 'I'll get you some dinner!'

Tim trotted out to the kitchen with her. Julian grinned at George. 'Well, look at that,' he said. 'Your mum's really nice, isn't she?'

'Yes – but I don't know what Dad'll say when he sees Tim in the house again,' said George, doubtfully.

Her father came back at that minute, looking very solemn. 'The police are taking all this very seriously,' he said, 'and so is my lawyer. They all think that you children have been incredibly clever and brave. And George – my lawyer says that the ingots definitely belong to us. Are there really a lot?'

'Dad! There are hundreds!' cried George. 'Absolutely hundreds – all in a big pile in the dungeon. Oh, Dad – are we rich now?'

'Yes,' said her father. 'Rich enough to give you and your mother all the things I've longed to give you for so many years and couldn't. I've worked hard – but it's not the kind of work that brings in a lot of money, and so I've become irritable and bad-tempered. But now you'll have everything you want!'

'I don't really want anything I haven't already got,' said George. 'But Dad, there's one thing I'd like more than anything else in the world – and it won't cost you a penny!'

'You shall have it!' said her father, putting his arm around George, much to her surprise. 'Just say what it is – and you shall have it!'

Just then they heard the pattering of big feet down the passage to the room they were in. A big hairy head pushed itself through the door and looked enquiringly at everyone there. It was Tim, of course!

Uncle Quentin stared at him in surprise. 'Isn't that Tim?' he asked. 'Hello, Tim!'

'Dad! Tim is the thing I want most in all the world,' said George, squeezing her father's arm. 'You wouldn't believe how wonderful he was on the island – and he wanted to fly at those men and fight them. Dad, I don't want any other present – I only want to keep Tim and have him here for my very own. We could afford to give him a proper kennel to sleep in now, and I'd see that he didn't disturb you, I really would.'

'Well, of course you can have him!' said her father – and Tim came right into the room at once, wagging his tail, looking as if he had understood every word that had been said. He actually licked Uncle Quentin's hand! Anne thought that was very brave of him.

But Uncle Quentin was quite different now. It seemed as if a great weight had been lifted off his shoulders. They were rich – George could go to a good school – and his wife could have the things he had so much wanted her to have – and he would be able to go on with the work he loved without feeling that he wasn't earning enough to keep his family in comfort. He beamed round at everyone, looking as friendly as anyone could wish!

George was overjoyed about Tim. She flung her arms round her father's neck and hugged him, something she had not done for a long time. He looked astonished but very pleased. 'Well,' he said, 'this is very nice. Oh – is that the police already?'

It was. They came up to the door and had a few words with Uncle Quentin. Then one stayed behind to take down the children's story in his notebook and the others went off to get a boat to the island.

The men had gone from there! The dinghy from the fishing-boat had taken them away – and now both dinghy and boat had disappeared! The motor-boat was still there, quite unusable. The inspector looked at it with a grin.

'Fierce young lady, isn't she, that Georgina?' he said. 'Done this job pretty well – no one could get away in this boat. We'll have to get it towed into harbour.'

The police brought back with them some of the ingots of gold to show Uncle Quentin. They had sealed up the door of the dungeon so that no one else could get in until the children's uncle was ready to go and fetch the gold. Everything was being done thoroughly and properly – though far too slowly for the children! They had hoped that the men would have been caught and taken to prison – and that the police would bring back all the gold at once!

They were all very tired that night and didn't

make any fuss at all when their aunt said that they must go to bed early. They undressed and then the boys went to eat their supper in the girls' bedroom. Tim was there, ready to lick up any fallen crumbs.

'We've had a wonderful adventure,' said Julian, sleepily. 'In a way I'm sorry it's ended – though at times I didn't enjoy it very much – especially when we were prisoners in that dungeon. That was awful.'

George was looking very happy as she nibbled her gingerbread biscuits. She grinned at Julian.

'And to think I hated the idea of you all coming here to stay!' she said. 'I was going to be so horrible to you! I was going to make you wish you were all home again! And now the only thing that makes me sad is the idea of you going away at the end of the holidays. And then, after having three friends with me, enjoying adventures like this, I'll be all on my own again. I've never felt lonely before – but I know I will now.'

'No, you won't,' said Anne, suddenly. 'You can do something that'll stop you being lonely ever again.'

'What?' said George in surprise.

'You can ask to go to the same boarding-school as I go to,' said Anne. 'It's a really friendly school – and we're allowed to keep our pets, so Tim could come too!'

'Really?' said George, her eyes shining. 'All right, I'll go. I always said I wouldn't – but now I see now how much better and happier it is to be with others than all by myself. And if I can have Tim, that just makes it perfect!'

'You'd better go back to your own room now, boys,' said Aunt Fanny, appearing at the doorway. 'Look at Dick, almost dropping with sleep! Well, you should all have pleasant dreams tonight. You've had an adventure to be proud of! George – is that Tim under your bed?'

'Oh! So it is!' said George, pretending to be surprised. 'Tim, what are you doing here?'

Tim crawled out and went over to George's mother. He lay flat on his tummy and looked up at her most appealingly out of his soft brown eyes.

'Do you want to sleep in the girls' room tonight?' said George's mother, with a laugh. 'All right – just for once!'

'*Mum*!' yelled George, overjoyed. 'Oh, thank

you, thank you, thank you! How did you guess that I just didn't want to be parted from Tim tonight? Oh, Mum! Tim, you can sleep on the rug over there.'

Four happy children snuggled down into their beds. Their wonderful adventure had come to a happy end. They had plenty of holidays still in front of them – and now that Uncle Quentin was no longer poor, he would be much more relaxed and friendly. George was going to school with Anne – and she had Tim at home again! The island and castle still belonged to George – everything was perfect!

'I'm so glad Kirrin Island wasn't sold, George,' said Anne, sleepily. 'I'm so glad it still belongs to you.'

'It belongs to three other people too,' said George. 'It belongs to me – and to you and Julian and Dick. I've discovered that it's fun to share things. So tomorrow I'm going to draw up a deed, or whatever it's called, and put in it that I give you and the others a quarter-share each. Kirrin Island and Castle will belong to us all!'

'Oh, George – how lovely!' said Anne, delighted. 'Won't the boys be pleased? I'm so ha . . .'

But before she could finish, the little girl was asleep. So was George. In the other room the two boys slept too, dreaming of ingots and dungeons and all kinds of exciting things.

Only one person was awake – and that was Tim. He had one ear up and was listening to the children's breathing. As soon as he knew they were asleep he got up quietly from his rug. He crept softly over to George's bed. He put his front paws up and sniffed at the sleeping girl.

Then, with a bound he was on the bed, and snuggled himself down into the crook of her legs. He gave a sigh, and shut his eyes. The four children might be happy – but Tim was happiest of all.

'Oh, Tim,' murmured George, half waking up as she felt him against her. 'Oh, Tim, you mustn't – but you do feel so nice. Tim – we'll have other adventures together, the five of us – won't we?'

They will – but that's another story!